BOOK ONE OF THE TREEBORN TRILOGY

Mapaline

RYAN J. SOUTHWORTH

Encourage Publishing
New Albany, Indiana

© Ryan J. Southworth, 2024

All rights reserved. Written permission must be secured from the publisher to use or reproduce any part of this book, except for brief quotations in reviews, endorsements, or articles.

Printed in the United States of America
For worldwide distribution.
Library of Congress Control Number 2024xxxxxx
Cataloging data:
Southworth, Ryan J.
Mapaline
The Treeborn Trilogy

1. Religion/Christian ministry/Children 2. Religion/Christian Living/Family & relationships 3. Religion/Christian Education/Children & Youth 4. Juvenile Fiction/Christian/Animals 5. Juvenile Fiction/Christian/Values and virtues 6. Juvenile Fiction/Activity Books/General 7. Family & relationships/School age

Cover and interior illustration by Adam Watkins

Edited by Julie Breihan

Interior and exterior design by Jonathan Lewis

MAPALINE: VOLUME 1 of the "Treeborn Trilogy" Series
ISBN 978-1-960166-04-3 (paperback)
ISBN 978-1-960166-16-6 (hardcover)

Other volumes in the "Treeborn Trilogy" Series
VOLUME 2: 978-1-960166-05-0 (paperback)
VOLUME 2: 978-1-960166-17-3 (hardcover)
VOLUME 3: 978-1-960166-06-7 (paperback)
VOLUME 3: 978-1-960166-18-0 (hardcover)

Published by:
Encourage Publishing, New Albany, Indiana
www.encouragepublishing.com

To my wife, who does not waver.

Contents

	Map of the Great Wilderness (with detail)	6
1	An Unusual Holiday	9
2	Tracks in the Snow	30
3	Thatch's Blunder	47
4	Danger at Mole Creek	69
5	A Peculiar Visitor	86
6	An Uncomfortable Conversation	109
7	Sighting at the Bee Tree	129
8	Thief in the Dark	145
9	The Signal	165
10	Mapaline's Stand	182
	Epilogue	202

About the Author	208
The Enchanting World of the Treeborn Trilogy	210
Map of the Great Wilderness	*212*

LAKE
GREENTIDE

BROOK HANDLE RIVER

THE GREAT
WILDERNESS

BULL RIVER

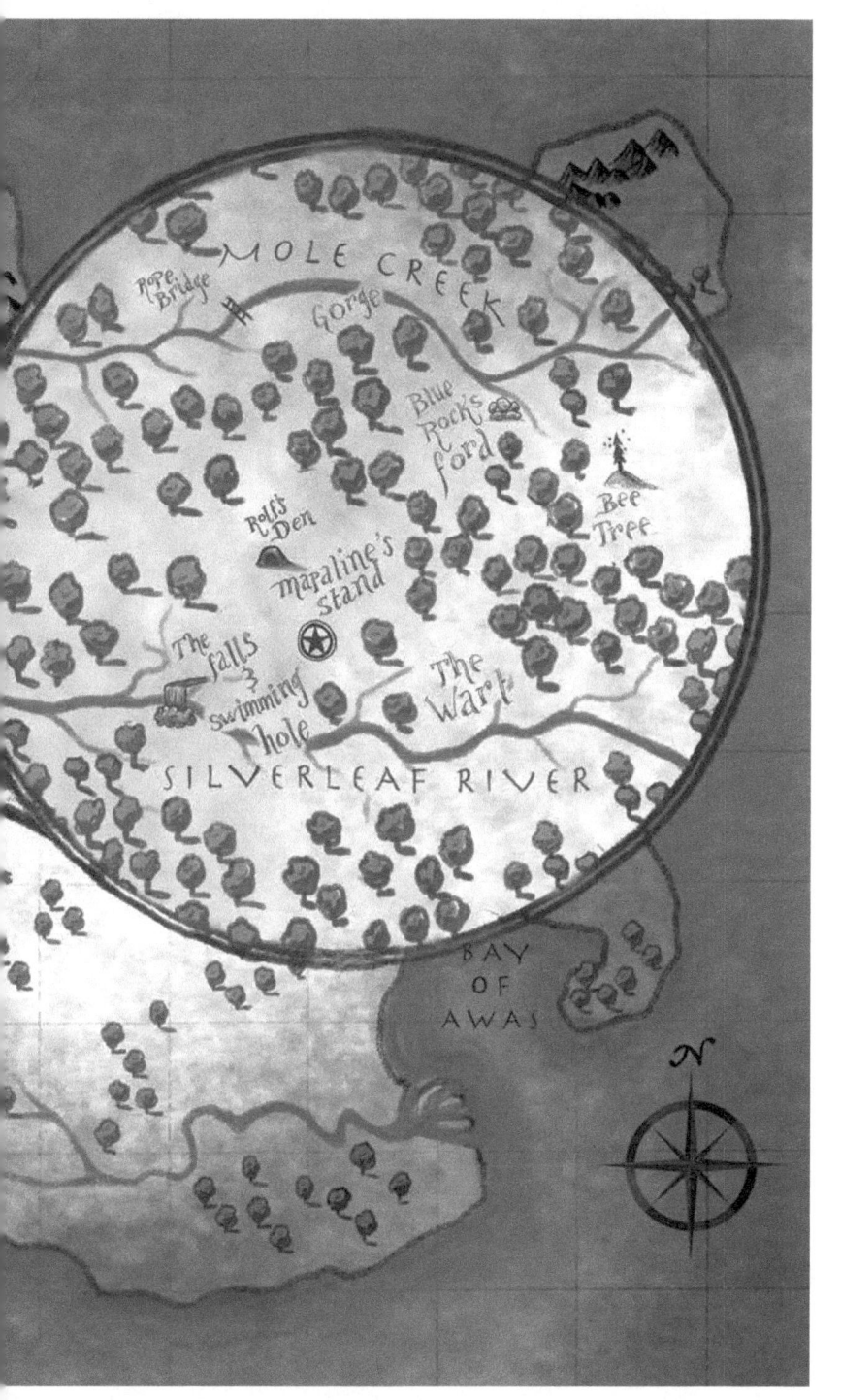

Dear Journal,

You'll never guess what happened today! i was out on an errand for Mama and i met someone very unusual. His name is Rolf . . .

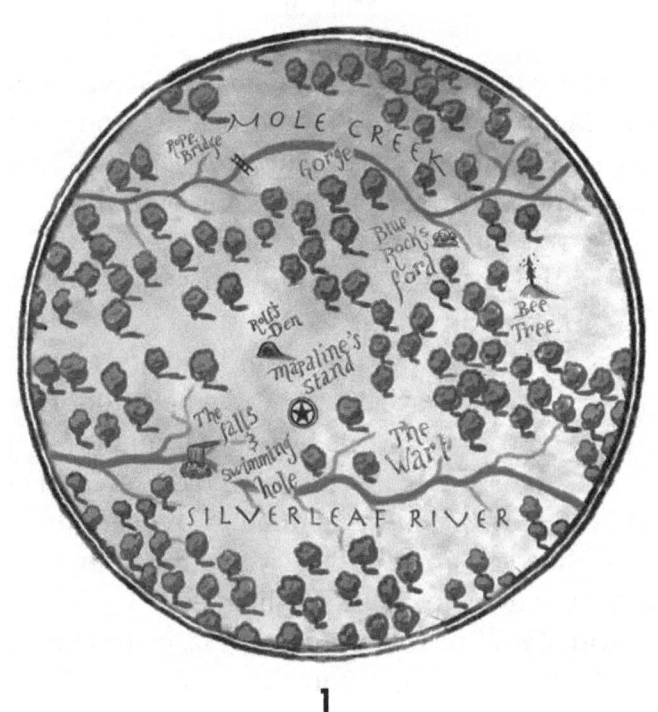

1

An Unusual Holiday

MAPALINE WAS A child, very much like yourself.

Well, perhaps not so *very* much. Unless you live in a deep, vast wilderness of forests and rivers and streams; unless you sleep in a small room, hung high up in the limbs of an old maple tree; unless you stand no taller than my kneecap and have hair that changes with the seasons, you are not so very much like Mapaline. She was a treeborn, and if you saw her you would think, *Isn't she a pretty little girl. But . . . somehow*—and you would feel silly saying it—*somehow she makes me think of a tree. Not very much, but still . . .*

I'm sure no one would think the same if they saw you, now, would they?

But if you are very curious and sometimes scared and sometimes brave; if you love to be outdoors with the sun on your back and the wind through your hair (of whatever sort) and find yourself drawn to cool water on hot days and warm, furry blankets on cold ones, then you are more like Mapaline than anyone *looking* at the two of you might guess.

And Mapaline had many friends, just as I'm sure you do. There was Briar from the maple tree alongside her own and Nettle from the fir tree across the way, and though they were older and tended to spend more time with her brother, Nut and Thatch Birch were friendly more often than not.

But Mapaline's best friend was Rolf.

Rolf, I am afraid, was nothing like any of your friends. Or mine. In fact, even if you knew a bear who was of the same enormous size and midnight black fur and wet, often sniffly nose, you would not come much closer to having a friend like Mapaline's, for her friend was a bear who could talk.

This, of course, for Mapaline's world, as for our own, was not normal. Talking animals were few and far between in the Great Wilderness, and just as likely to be cruel and evil as kind and warmhearted. Thankfully, Rolf was the latter kind, and ever since Mapaline had found him nosing through the springtime soil in search of roots and bugs and old, forgotten acorns, they had been fast friends.

Mapaline was especially glad for Rolf on days like today, far from the new warmth of spring, when snow was on the ground and a cold wind rattled the bare branches overhead. Rolf's den was not nearly as neat and clean as Mapaline's home, as Rolf was not nearly the housekeeper that Mama Maple was. But tucked down in the dark den, with the smells of the wet dirt and exposed roots and dry grass bedding, and up against Rolf's thick fur, it was about the nicest place Mapaline had ever been.

She was almost asleep when Rolf said, "It will be dark soon, Mapaline."

"Yes," she said, and though he was right and she really needed to be heading up the hill to her stand, the thought of leaving this snuggly nest for the blowing cold was not a pleasant one. "Maybe I should just sleep here tonight," she suggested and closed her eyes again.

"*Hmmnnnmmrrm*," Rolf grumbled, and the sound was something between a laugh and a growl. "Your parents are not overly fond of me and would be less fond still if I kept you from home all the winter night long."

Mapaline scowled at this and knew he was right, but did not open her eyes.

"And I think your mother is needing your help preparing for Short Day tomorrow."

"Humpf," Mapaline said in her best talking-bear

voice. "I much prefer the eating and dancing of Short Day to the cooking and trimming."

Mapaline still didn't open her eyes, though now, at Rolf's reminder of her duties for tomorrow's shortest-day-of-the-year holiday, she felt a pinprick of guilt and responsibility in her stomach. It is the same, I'm sure, as you feel when your mother has told you to clean up your room and you haven't yet begun or your father has warned you about eating too many cookies and you find that you've taken three or four instead of one or two.

Still, it was terribly comfortable in the warm dark and perhaps Mama Maple wouldn't miss her too much and . . . Rolf suddenly stiffened and then rolled from side to side to get himself to his feet, and Mapaline's mind was made up for her. It was either leave the den or be buried beneath an avalanche of black fur and bear belly.

Out she went.

Mapaline shivered in the falling snow and thought longingly of the spring when her hair would grow back with the new buds and blossoms. For now, she quickly pulled her thick hood up over her bald head. Rolf nudged her out farther and then, after buttoning up her squirrel-skin coat, she climbed atop his back and they were on their way, trudging up the hill. If you have never ridden on the back of a large black bear through freshly fallen snow, I cannot say that I would recommend it. In your case or mine, it might mean that we were very shortly going to be eaten. But in Mapaline's case, the soft *tromp, tromp* of Rolf's paws and the warmth of his body as she dug herself deep into his coat made the climb to her home far more enjoyable than walking would have been.

As they crested the hill to the flat ground where the trees of Mapaline's stand grew, the sun was just touching the flat, western horizon and the second of three moons was just peeking in the east. All three would rise this Short Day—even the little Water Moon—and would make for a bright night reflecting off all the snow. Still, there was a hustle and a bustle going on as other little treeborn rushed about to make final outdoor preparations before the dim night came upon them. In the open lawn between the circle of hometrees, a long wooden table had been set and nearby was the Short Day pole, strung with rope and colorful dancing flags. There were smells twirling in the cold, sharp air, of roasted hazelnuts and simmering squirrel and the last of the year's candied fruit.

These smells, to you and me, who are more accustomed to turkey and potatoes and cranberry sauce, would have been pleasant, but a bit odd. To Mapaline they were the smells of a long-anticipated celebration, the turning of the sun and stars from long winter toward a coming spring. She could not help but smile, even knowing, as she did, that she would be awake for some hours more helping her mother finish preparing the feast.

To Rolf . . . Oh, poor Rolf. You see, however strong and moving these smells might be to you or me or

Mapaline, they were doubly strong—triply strong!—to the sensitive snout of a bear. In truth, he'd smelled the first hints of beechnut pie all the way down the hill in his dark den and now, standing so close, it was all he could do to keep his mouth from hanging open and the drool from falling, frozen, to the ground.

Mapaline felt his stomach gurgle and growl as she slid from his back.

"Mapaline!"

The little girl turned to see her mother and father hanging a string of holly berries from the lower boughs of a nearby fir tree. They smiled and waved and smiled again, this time as you might smile when your best friend arrives at a party but has brought their troublesome younger brother with them. Or when your sweet aunt and uncle arrive for Christmas but have brought along that cousin who plays rough with your toys and breaks them.

"Oh, and . . . hello . . . Rolf," said Mapaline's mother.

"Sorry I'm late, Mama," Mapaline called. "It was so cold today we decided to take a rest in Rolf's den and I almost fell asleep."

"Oh, my . . . yes . . . Rolf's den. Well, I *was* beginning to worry, Mape. And we need your help cooking tonight. The boys have been out hunting up snowberries and nuts and . . . Um . . ."

Mama trailed off, a half smile frozen to her face, and Mapaline realized that Rolf had forgotten to keep his mouth closed. He was staring up at the nearest hometree and gaping at the smell of a winter stew that drifted down from one of the rooms.

"Rolf!" Mapaline whispered. She elbowed him, and

An Unusual Holiday

though her elbow didn't reach even halfway up his leg, it was enough to remind him to close his mouth. "You're scaring my mother again."

Mapaline's parents were not quite sure what to do about Rolf. It was obvious that Mapaline loved him, and she'd now spent so much time rambling the Wilderness with him that they more or less trusted that the bear was safe and would take good care of their only daughter. But . . . Rolf was so *big*! And bears were usually *dangerous*. And the fact that he was a talking bear was just so . . . *odd*. Imagine your own mother or father letting you take a walk down the street with a talking alligator. Or a singing tiger. It wasn't normal, and so whenever Mapaline talked about Rolf or went off with him on a midday romp down to the river, they felt that confusing feeling inside their stomachs that was a bit like butterflies and a bit like the stomach flu.

Rolf pulled his snout away from the smell and found Mapaline's mother staring at him from nearby and her father, farther back, scowling as he always did when Rolf was around.

"Sorry, Mother Maple," Rolf said, and then he tried to smile but this did not help much. A bear's smile is only slightly less frightening than a bear's snarl, and both show far too many teeth to set anyone at ease. "I was just, um, enjoying the thought of food. Your food, I mean. I mean, the food you all are preparing."

"Oh dear," was all she could say, but then, as Rolf whispered a soft good night to Mapaline and turned to go, Mapaline's mother did something very unexpected. Very unexpected indeed. It was something so unexpected that it took a few moments for everyone to realize what she'd done and for Rolf to turn back, bushy eyebrows raised, and ask in a very confused, very beary voice, "What did you say, Mother Maple?"

"I said, well, I was just thinking that . . . Short Day is such a lovely time and we always have far too much food and . . . well, if Reed Maple knows anything, he knows the weather and he said it was shaping up to be especially cold tomorrow, and I know it can be difficult even for a bear of your . . . um . . . strength . . . er . . . size to find enough food when it's been so cold. So I was wondering if you might like to join our stand. For the holiday. Tomorrow."

Rolf didn't move. Mapaline didn't move. Mapaline's father didn't move except that his frown grew deeper and his eyes more squinty.

Then Mapaline's mother said, "Oh dear," very softly and tried to pretend she was busy hanging more garland.

Mapaline was the first to find her voice. She had been inviting her best friend to join the stand for dinners and celebrations and games ever since she met him, but as it was obvious that his presence made some quite uncomfortable, he always refused.

"Rolf! Will you come? Please, you must come. It will be the greatest Short Day ever!"

Rolf squinted an eye and gave a sort of a growl. Not a real growl, certainly, but a mumbling, rumbling, ruminating kind of growl. He looked over again at Mapaline's father and then back up at the window of the room from which all the rich, delicious smells were coming.

Now, Rolf was a very special bear. Most obviously,

he could talk, but he was special in other ways as well, some that Mapaline was just beginning to understand and some of which she had no idea. But mixed up with all that "special" there was a part of him that was very much like a regular, walk-through-the-woods-and-eat-honey-and-scratch-your-back-on-a-tree bear, and that part had an extremely difficult time saying no to delicious smells and the food they lead to.

"*Grrmmmmrrrr*," he said finally. "Thank you, Mother Maple. I think I will come."

Mapaline squealed and jumped up as high as she could jump to hug her friend.

Her mother said, "Oh dear" again, and her father kept on scowling.

REED MAPLE WAS right. All night long the cold winter got colder and the wind windier and the snow very much snowier. No light from the moons could pierce the storm clouds, and when morning came, it came only as a diffused and subtle glow. When Mapaline woke, the long table outside and all the garlands and trimmings were coated with a thick crust of snow. The Short Day pole, tall to the treeborn, but to you or me not so very tall, was half buried. All the windows in the stand, open last night for the heat of the baking and the cooking, were shut tight, leaving only the smell of chimney smoke in the cold woods.

Mapaline was up early.

Think how you feel on Christmas Eve. Excited and nervous and warm and giggly. Now imagine that on *this* Christmas, your very best friend in the whole world is coming to visit and spend the entire day with you, feasting and dancing and playing.

That's how Mapaline had felt all night long and now, since she hadn't slept much anyway, she rolled out of her bed and into a warm robe and little mouse-fur slippers and ran to her door. She had to push hard against the icy snow and hold tight as she climbed down the slippery branches to her parents' room, which hung lower down on the tree than her own. By the time she got to the door, her twiggy fingers were quite cold and she was wishing that her head, like the Firs' and the Pines' and the Hollies', was covered with hair all winter long.

"It's very cold!" she said as she swung down and through the doorway. Her mother and father were awake and sitting around the family table, as close to the crackling fireplace as they could scoot.

"Where are Red and Aker?" Mapaline asked. "Aren't they up yet? It's Short Day!"

"Mapaline—"

"Should I go wake them? They'll miss the maple rolls!" Mapaline was talking very fast and very loud, just as you probably talk when you run into your parents' bedroom to wake them for presents and Christmas breakfast. She was so excited that she hadn't yet noticed the half-eaten maple rolls on the table and the wooden cups half filled with sweet tea and the wet handkerchief clutched in her mother's hand. "I spent hours making the rolls last night and they're going to miss them. The maple syrup is always best warm. Where are they? Do we have to wait for them?"

An Unusual Holiday

"Mapaline," Papa Maple said. "Mapaline, I'm afraid that Short Day has been canceled."

"Canceled?" Mapaline stopped, and like warmth driven away by a cold wind, all that exciting, Short Day morning feeling left her in an instant. "What do you mean?"

"Moose Birch and Ever Fir came by early this morning. It's too cold for anyone to be outside today, Mape. Frightfully cold. The snow's hard and icy, and it's still coming down in blankets. It would be impossible to have an outdoor feast and certainly too dangerous to have everyone running around for dances."

"But I was just outside," Mapaline said, and she could feel a few tears coming to her eyes. "It's not *that* cold. We could make a fire. A great bonfire like last Short Day. Couldn't we?"

"All the wood set aside for the bonfires is frozen over, Mapaline." Mama Maple dabbed at a few tears in her own eyes. "It would take hours to dig it out, and maybe hours more to get a fire started in this bitter cold. Red and Aker were already down and went back up to their room once we told them. They were very upset."

"But . . . but . . . Rolf was going to come today," Mapaline said, and at the thought of her friend and how disappointed he would be and how disappointed she was that he couldn't come, she really began to cry. This, of course, embarrassed her, which made her angry, and before her mother could offer her a warm roll and some tea to make her feel better, she was back out the door and climbing up to her room.

It *was* that cold and the wind was biting and bitter.

By the time she reached her room, she was shivering, and it took some time buried beneath the thick blankets on her bed for her to warm up and be able to cry herself to sleep.

Mapaline slept for a while and then woke up and remembered that Short Day was canceled and then cried again and fell back to sleep. When she woke a few hours later, a maple roll and a cup of lukewarm tea were sitting on the little table next to her bed. Someone had stoked the fire in her hearth and the room was warm and cozy.

"Humph," she said and scowled her most angry scowl. She was, you understand, not really angry at her mother or father. She wasn't really even angry at Moose Birch or Ever Fir, who had probably been the first to recommend canceling. She was just . . . well . . . *angry*. Angry that things were not turning out as she had hoped they would. You know how she felt. Remember that one time, when you had that great and wonderful plan, and everyone was going to be there and enjoy it and everything was going to be just right and perfect and then . . . it wasn't. Remember how you felt that day? Well, that's just how Mapaline felt, and she couldn't really explain it but she wanted to be mad at somebody or something.

She nibbled at the maple roll, which was really very good, and then sipped the tea. Her small room had two windows, one to the east and one to the west, and she crossed the cold floorboards in her slippers to see if the sun had broken through the winter clouds. It had not. But for the few bright, stiff flags standing out from the strings around the Short Day pole and the black, bare trunks of the trees, there was nothing but white and gray all around her stand and on down the hill toward the river in the gorge below. White and gray, gray and white, the clouds still rolling and the snow still falling. None of this made her feel any better.

The door scraped open and a blast of winter came into the room with her mother.

"You're awake," Mama Maple said and snuggled up close beside Mapaline near the window. "Did you get the roll and the tea I left you?"

Mapaline nodded but could not quite bring herself to give a cheerful answer. She was not *feeling* cheerful and didn't want to give the wrong impression.

"I know you're upset about Rolf."

Mapaline sniffled and nodded again.

"Do you want to talk about it?"

Mapaline did want to talk about it, but at the same time she very much didn't. A part of her wanted to stay grumpy because, somehow, being grumpy and staying grumpy and making those around you grumpy sort of makes you feel better, doesn't it?

But mothers know this, and so Mama Maple just waited. Eventually Mapaline said, "I was really looking forward to having him come for the day. He's never done that before."

"I know. I was looking forward to it too."

Mapaline looked up at her mother's bald head and lined skin and smiling, sad face. "You were?"

Mapaline

"Well, yes . . . I mean . . . I knew it would make you happy. And I thought, well, I thought that maybe I should get to know Rolf a little bit . . . you know, better. So I don't feel so nervous around him all the time."

"Rolf shouldn't make you nervous, Mama. He's very kind."

"Yes. I'm sure that's true. But he's also very big."

Mapaline giggled, just a little, and then she saw him.

Down below and coming into the clearing was the large, furry hind end of Rolf the bear. He was walking backward, swinging from side to side, and then Mapaline realized that he was dragging something into the open space next to the snow-covered table and Short Day pole.

"What's he doing?" her mother asked.

"It looks like . . ."

"Oh my goodness!" Mama said, and then Mapaline was throwing on her thick coat and tall boots and fuzzy mittens and was out the door. She almost slipped twice coming down the tree, and by the time she came up through the blowing snow to Rolf's side, the bear had gotten the huge carcass of a freshly killed deer up on the table.

The wind was loud and swirling and Mapaline had to shout to be heard. "Rolf! What's this?"

Her friend swung his big muzzle around to face her and grinned, which was more frightening than he intended. But Mapaline was used to it.

"I thought," he said in his deep, slow voice, "that since your stand was so nice to invite me to your celebration, I should bring something for the feast."

An Unusual Holiday

"It's a deer! A whole deer!"

Rolf stood back, breathing heavily from the effort of dragging the deer all the way up the hill. "Well, yes," he said. "Your family eats deer. Don't they?"

"Yes!" Mapaline's face was starting to hurt, as much from smiling as from the cold. She was not feeling grumpy now at all. "They're just so . . . big! We're almost never able to hunt them in winter. Where did you . . . How did you . . ."

Rolf shrugged his big bear shoulders and tried to look humble and nonchalant, as if it had been nothing, really. Nothing at all to track down and overcome a large buck and then drag it through the woods and the blizzard to bring it for the feast.

Mapaline hugged his leg and then remembered. "But, Rolf, Short Day's been canceled. The storm's too bad."

Rolf seemed not to have noticed until now that there was no one else in the clearing and that there were no yummy smells coming from the tightly shuttered hometrees. He looked around and sniffed the air sadly.

"*Humph*," he growled. "What about a fire? Wouldn't a few big fires warm up the clearing enough for the feast?"

"All the wood for the bonfires is buried under the ice and snow."

Rolf stood still for a moment, quiet and thinking, and Mapaline watched him. She could tell that an idea was forming behind his big, black eyes, possibly a good idea, and she didn't want to interrupt him. With Rolf there she suddenly had a feeling that perhaps, just perhaps, there was a way to fix this terrible, awful, disappointing Short Day. She didn't know how, just as you don't know how your mother or father can possibly fix one of your own terrible, awful, disappointing days, but somehow you know they can, because they're grown-ups and they love you and they can do things that you can't even imagine.

Mapaline had learned that Rolf was like that, and as she stood there watching, she felt that maybe this day would end better than it had begun.

Rolf was still so long that the snow began gathering on his back and then he looked down at Mapaline with a bit of a scowl.

"*Hmmrrmmm*," he growled and then let out a long sigh. "Very well. Show me where the wood is."

"The wood?" Mapaline said, and this was not the wonderful plan that she had been expecting (it never is, you know). She led him over to the great pile of branches and limbs and twigs that the stand had been gathering for weeks. There was enough wood to make quite the bonfire, even for normal-sized people like you or me, and there were two other similar piles at opposite ends of the clearing. But unlike the small catches of firewood that the treeborn kept protected for use in their own homes, these great woodpiles were exposed to the weather and now hidden by a layer of ice and snow.

Rolf looked at the white pile for a few moments with a scowl on his face and a grumbling, rumbling noise coming from his throat. Then he turned and scanned the frosted rooms hung here and there all along the

An Unusual Holiday

edge of the clearing, half hidden behind the swirling snow and closed tight against the cold. Ribbons of smoke rose from every chimney, but other than that there was no sign that anyone else was even awake.

"Mapaline," he said. "Stand over there and turn around."

Mapaline walked to where his snout had pointed and turned her back to the snowy mound. "What are you doing?" she asked.

For a moment Rolf didn't say anything. Then, so quietly that she almost couldn't hear him, he said, "Don't ask how, Mapaline. All right? You must not ask."

"How what, Rolf? What do you mean?"

"Just don't ask how," he said again, and then there was a sound like a deep, long, strong breath and another like a deep, long, menacing growl and Mapaline felt something very strange. Her front side — her face and knees and hands clasped across her chest — was still very cold. So cold that her nose and cheeks stung and her clothes felt stiff against her skin. But the back of her began to feel very different. Her fur coat began to feel soft again and her skin warm and toasty beneath it.

Mapaline whirled around and found all three piles of wood ablaze, with red and orange flames reaching high up to melt the snowflakes that continued to fall. Mapaline was, of course, more than surprised and began to say, "How?" but then remembered Rolf's words and bit her tongue. It was very difficult not to ask. Can you imagine it, to have seen something like this and to have your best friend know the secret and not be able to ask him to tell you? For a moment it nearly drove her wild and she almost asked despite his warning. But she didn't.

Instead, to herself, she thought, *Rolf is certainly not a normal bear, is he?*

THE BONFIRES WERE big and hot, and soon three circles of snow had melted and the table was thawing and the Short Day pole was more or less freed. Mapaline got her father and her father got Moose Birch and Ever Fir and they got some of the others from the stand and soon the deer was being dressed and spitted and roasted over a few smaller fires begun for just that purpose. Soon, despite the weather, which was still very cold and very snowy, other treeborn began to come out of their homes and make their way down to stand and talk and laugh within the warmth of the fires. And then they left and came back again with all those delicious smells from the day before and the delicious foods that were attached to them. Before Mapaline knew it, there was a different but wonderful kind of Short Day celebration going on, with all the hustle and bustle and eating and drinking, and even some of the dancing, happening within the glow of the fires.

All the while, Rolf sat off to the side, trying not to smile too broadly but making happy, rumbling sorts of noises as he watched all the excitement. At first the treeborn didn't know what to do about him. They all knew who he was, and most felt, as Mapaline's parents did, that he was odd and good but made

An Unusual Holiday

them frightfully nervous. Then, after half an hour or so, Mama Maple walked over and laid a plate full of maple rolls on the snow in front of him.

"Mapaline made these," she said. "Thank you, Rolf. Thank you so much for coming and for . . . well . . ." She paused a moment and then began, "How did you—" but Rolf cut her off gently.

"Please, Mother Maple, please," he said. And then again with just a touch of beary gruffness, "Please don't ask how."

And no one did, not even when Mapaline brought over her friends Briar and Nettle, or when her brothers came over with the Birch boys. Not even when they began to bring him a steady stream of breads and pies and stews and venison or when he began to give rides around the Short Day pole. As you might expect, Mapaline was the first to take a ride, for no one else was brave enough, but then another summoned up the courage to climb his fur and perch atop his shoulders, and after that, others became brave as well. By the time the fires were burning low and it was growing too cold to be outside again, Rolf had given rides to more than half of all the treeborn in Mapaline's stand, including, if you can believe it, Mama Maple.

When it was finally time for Rolf to leave, there were far more friendly "goodbyes" than there had been "hellos," and I think it is safe to say that almost everyone hoped that he would return again soon. Mapaline assured them that he would. Everyone agreed that this had certainly been the most unusual Short Day in memory and that it had been wonderful despite the storm. Everyone also agreed, though not in public and not very loudly, that Rolf was a very strange bear.

A very strange bear indeed.

Dear Journal,

i don't think i have ever felt as completely tired as i do right now. i might fall asleep any minute. But it has been such a day! i've never seen the stand so completely happy as they were tonight and with a bear on the green, no less! And i was so happy too! Rolf was wonderful and everyone loved him!

But now that everyone's gone home, i feel . . . i don't know. Strange. it's the first day of the year, and for some reason it feels different than before. Perhaps it's because this is the last short day that Aker will still be considered a sprout. Or because everyone is saying that they've never seen a winter begin so early and so cold? And then there's Rolf. He's amazing, but . . . how did he do that!?

i've the feeling that it's going to be a very unusual year.

Mapaline

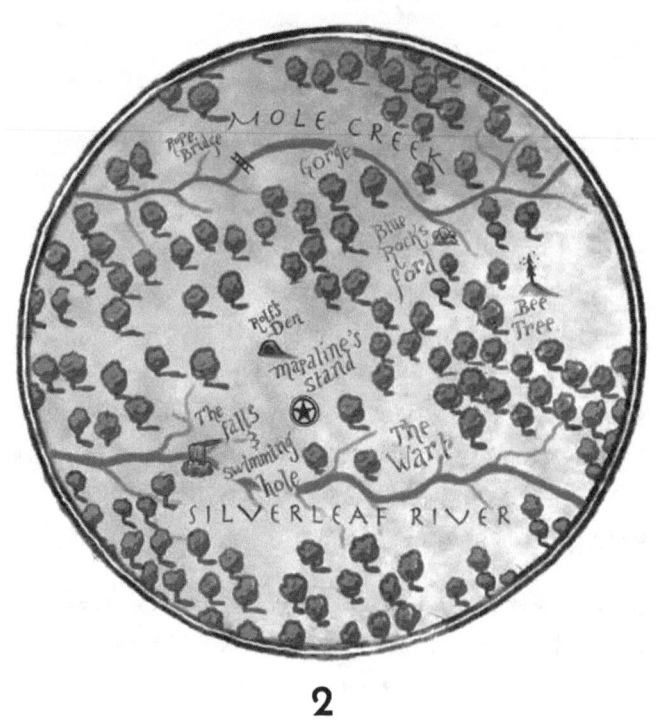

2

Tracks in the Snow

THOUGH THE SNOW stopped the day after Short Day, the cold did not and the winter, which had begun innocently enough, soon became the coldest that anyone in the stand could remember. Even old Caddo Maple, who had founded the stand before any of the rest of them were even sprouts, could not recall a more biting cold than that which greeted them each morning.

When first one, then two, and then three weeks of this had passed, Mapaline and her brothers decided they'd had enough. The very thought of spending one more day cooped up in their rooms, feeding fires and playing dice and cards, was enough to make them want to jump up and down and scream out for the boredom of it. It's how you and I get sometime late in February, when spring is coming and the long winter stretches out behind us. When we've been stuck indoors for months and months and want nothing more than to run through the grass in our bare feet and swing on the playground and swim in the lake.

Only for Mapaline and the treeborn it was worse. First because their hometree rooms were very small and cramped, and second because it was *not* late winter with spring right around the corner. It was just past Short Day, and the winter would be with them for many weeks more. During a normal winter they would be out-of-doors as much as possible, sledding and snowshoeing and skating, but with the weather so dangerously cold they were forced to keep inside except for the chores that absolutely had to be done.

But not today. Today Mapaline and her older brother, Aker, and her younger brother, Red, were bundling up in all the coats and warm socks and hats and scarves that they could find, and they were going down to the pool to try and skate on the ice. They knew they would have to clear off plenty of snow and that by the end of the morning they would probably be very cold and stiff and miserable, but at the moment they didn't care. They just needed to get out. Out!

So down the hill they tromped, past the tall, bare trees and climbing over the branches that had fallen across the trail and would have to be cleared in the spring. A deep gorge ran between their hill and another rising up on the opposite side, and a narrow river tumbled down its length. Its name was the Silverleaf, and away downstream, where the hills lowered and the gorge became shallower, there was a small waterfall and a wide pool that was perfect for swimming in the summer and for ice skating in the winter.

Well, most winters. The three treeborn soon realized that there would be no clearing off the hard, crusty snow for skating this year. It would have taken all day long, and after all their hard work the ice would be too rough and bumpy to skate on anyway. So they decided to look for ice caves instead.

Finding ice caves was a familiar winter game. It was not quite as fun as sledding or skating, but it was much more fun than going back to their rooms and playing even a second more of cards. Anything was more fun than that. The first cave was easy: the waterfall that formed the swimming pool froze solid almost every winter and the little treeborn could wiggle their way back behind the wall of ice. This was one of the nice things about being so small. It would be very difficult for you or me to ever find an ice cave large enough for us to fit into. How many waterfalls that large do *you* know of? But for the treeborn, there were ice caves all over, and for all the cold they were beautiful places to find.

This specific cave was very familiar to them. In the summer there was a shelf of rock they could sit on behind the falling water, and they and their friends often hid treasures in the crevices. Mapaline looked for them now, but the bits and bobbles she found were frozen hard to the rock. She ran her hands over the rippling ice wall and looked through it to the distorted world on the other side.

"This is boring," Red said suddenly. "We see this cave all the time. Let's go look for a new one."

Aker and Mapaline agreed. Out they went, across the river, and soon they were crisscrossing the slopes of the hill on the other side.

Now, you might be thinking, *Where are these children's parents? Should they be tramping off all on their own? What if they get lost?*

These, I'm afraid, are questions fit only for the places you and I live. In our cities or towns, children simply do not set off on an adventure by themselves. There are too many dangers, too many other people—some of whom are very scary—and far too many roads to cross. It was not so for the treeborn. First off, there were no roads to speak of and, even if there had been, no cars that might run them over. Second, there were no other people in this part of the Great Wilderness. The nearest treeborn stand was three days away and they did not visit one another often. Third, there was small chance of getting lost because all treeborn, from the youngest sprouts to the ancient roots, were so used to the woods that moving from here to there for them was like you or me walking from our bedroom to the bathroom in the middle of the day.

So up the hill they went without giving it even a thought.

THEY DID NOT find much. It turns out that ice caves, like children, do not appreciate such bitter cold. In order for the long icicle bars to grow and lengthen to form the caves, some of the snow must melt and refreeze and melt and refreeze again. As it was, the weather was so utterly cold that nothing was melting at all.

By the time they reached the crest of the hill and had unsuccessfully checked several promising spots, Red had begun a string of complaints.

"I'm cold!" he said in his little sprout voice.

"I know, Red," Mapaline said. "But at least we're not stuck indoors, right?"

"But this is boring," he whined again.

"Maybe we'll find something up at the point. There are always some ice caves up at the point."

They walked a few steps farther up the length of the ridge.

"I'm cold!" Red said again.

And so it went. For a very long half hour the three treeborn trudged and stumbled and slipped their way through the hard snow, the wind at their back and Red complaining all the way. I find it hard to blame him.

I'm sorry to say that Mapaline and Aker did not feel altogether as understanding.

"Red, if you don't be quiet, I'm going to throw you into a snowbank," Aker said.

This was not very kind, but it did quiet Red, and at the moment Aker was not *feeling* very kind. Perhaps the kind part of him had frozen. The cold can do that, I think.

They walked in silence for a while. The wind picked up and was frightfully biting. It began to snow, and whatever sun there had been disappeared behind thick clouds, as if it, too, was cold and needed to snuggle under a heavy blanket. They reached the overhang of rocks at the point and found not a beautiful, encouraging, that-sure-makes-the-miserable-walk-worth-it ice cave, but a few pitiful icicles frozen to the face of the stone. They stood there for a moment, staring and shivering.

Then, would you believe it? I'm sure you can. A grumble slipped from Mapaline's mouth as well.

"I *am* cold!" she said. "Red's right, this is boring."

Red mumbled something through his thick scarf, and though it was hard to make out the words, I think it's safe to assume that his kind part was frozen as well.

"You guys are just seedlings," Aker said, which is the same as you or me calling someone a baby. Then a gust of wind roared up and over the hillcrest, right into all their faces, and suddenly Aker didn't think they were seedlings after all. As a matter of fact, a whine *almost* escaped his own mouth before he caught it and swallowed it back down.

"Well," he said instead, "if we go back, it's only to be stuck in our rooms again. I'm not sure which is worse."

"This is worse!" both Red and Mapaline said at once, and Aker could not argue. Though he was older and more mature and better at self-control, he found that complaints were trying to escape his lips as well and finally, though he gave it a serious fight, one slipped out.

"This *is* miserable," he said. "And stupid. Let's go home."

That was that.

The three treeborn turned downhill. Oh, what a sour group they were now: tired, cold, and with all their kind and helpful parts frozen as solid as the ice. What's more, though their rooms in the maple tree would be warm, they would also be stuffy and tiresome, and that offered little hope of improving their moods. From their scowling mouths came first a flurry and then a full-blown blizzard of groans and bellyaches. It was frightful to hear even if you couldn't understand exactly what they were saying through their scarves.

There is really no excuse for this. You and I have been there too, I'm sure, but I'm afraid that all three of them were thinking only of themselves and that not a few of their gripes were directed toward each other; things like, "Whose dumb idea was this anyway?" and "It's Aker's fault we didn't find any ice caves" and "Wasn't it Mapaline's job to remember to bring some snacks?"

In those first few minutes on their way down the hill, they each said some things they would certainly have regretted later. Undoubtedly, that night they would have all taken turns apologizing and saying how sorry they were for acting so selfishly and rude. That's always the way, isn't it? If only we would remember to stop our poor behavior *before* we have to apologize for it.

In this case, however, there would be no apologies, and that is because something happened to make them forget all their morning miseries.

I MUST WARN you that this part is a bit frightening. If you are reading this right before bed, you may want to stop for the evening and pick it up again tomorrow. Think about it. I'm serious.

Well, I guess you've made your decision.

About halfway down the hill, Aker, who was leading their unfortunate procession, stopped short. The others came up and gathered around him.

"Look at that," he said and pointed down at the ground.

Mapaline and Red looked. There in the snow was a set of footprints, coming up from the river and trailing past them and over the crest of the hill. Footprints were nothing spectacular. All three of the children, even little Red, knew all the footprints of all the different kinds of animals that lived in their part of the Great Wilderness. They could track them and tell how fresh the prints were and even guess how large and healthy the animal was. It was second nature to them, like you or me knowing how to turn on the television or use the microwave . . . except that their skills were much more interesting.

But this was different.

"What . . . Is that a fox?" Red asked.

Aker shook his head. "Too large for a fox. And look here, at these claw prints. Not like a fox at all."

"What is it then? I've never seen these before. Is it a wolf?"

"No," Aker said, and the tone of his voice was serious. None of them were thinking of the cold anymore. "Mapaline, do you know?"

Mapaline nodded her head. She knew. At least, she thought she knew, though she hoped she was wrong.

"It's a wolverine," she said quietly.

Aker nodded. "Fresh too. I'll bet it came by this morning."

This was not good news. Even Red, who had never seen wolverine prints before, and Mapaline, who had never seen a live wolverine, knew that the wolverine was to be feared far more than the predators that more commonly lived nearby. Wolves were dangerous, but they could not climb trees and were easy enough to escape. Bears could climb but were too big to follow the little treeborn into all the tight nooks and crannies that they could fit into, and the smaller hunters like the fox and rattlesnake would not typically attack something as fierce as a treeborn.

But the wolverine. Oh dear. They climbed trees. They could fit into many small caves and crevices. They were smart enough to wait in ambush for a passing meal and ferocious enough to fight a treeborn to the very end. There were even stories of wolverines climbing hometrees and breaking into rooms to eat the sleeping treeborn within.

Tracks in the Snow

I told you that this part was scary. If you and I are set on edge just *hearing* about these dangerous beasts, think how the treeborn felt! But you've read this far and you can't stop now.

"We'd better get home," Aker said, and the three of them stepped quickly in and around the deep prints and started back down the hill. But then, after only a few steps, Aker stopped again. There in the snow, running right alongside the first set of prints, was a second set, just as deep and fresh as the first. Not one, but *two* wolverines. Two!

"I've never heard of two wolverines traveling together," Aker said, and this put more shivers into the children than any amount of snow and cold could do.

"Let's hurry," Mapaline said, and as they continued down the hill, their thoughts were not nearly so selfish as they had been before. They held close together, hand in hand, eyes up and watching over each other lest they be surprised and eaten.

Yes, that's right. I said it: *eaten*. If you are like me, you have been thinking how nice it would be to be a treeborn. To live in a great treehouse and wake up to the sun coming through woods and over mountains instead of buildings and highways. To drink from a fresh stream and go fishing for your dinner and munch wild raspberries by a campfire at night. And it *would* be wonderful. Life in our world can seem cramped and smelly by comparison.

Tracks in the Snow

But you and I never have to worry about being eaten. That, I think, makes the cars and buildings and televisions seem, perhaps, not so bad after all.

You can imagine that Mapaline and her brothers walked as quickly as they could through the snow. After just a minute or so, however, they were brought up short again, not by another set of footprints, but by a voice.

"Mapaline!" The call was deep and a bit rough and came from the top of the ridge behind them. You might guess who it was, and if you do, you will feel immediately better knowing that he was nearby.

"Rolf!" Mapaline said, and there he was, a great black bear standing at the top of the ridge. The three children immediately turned back *up* the hill and headed for their friend. As much as they had wanted to be safe in their hometree a moment ago, they now felt that being near Rolf would be safer still. Somehow, though they had never seen Mapaline's friend in a fight or even seen him angry, they knew that two wolverines would not be a match for such a bear as Rolf. After a few moments they stood at the top of the hill, near enough to him that he helped to block the wind.

"What are you children doing out here in the cold?" Rolf asked. His face was very grave.

"We were going to go skating down at the pool, but the snow was too hard and deep for us to clear off the ice," Mapaline said. "Then we were looking for ice caves, but couldn't find any. Then we were heading for home when we came across wolverine tracks!"

"Two sets of them," Red added, and he could not help but look nervously over his shoulder.

Rolf nodded. "I saw them as well."

"Have you ever seen two together, Rolf?" Aker asked.

"*Mmmnnrrmmn*," Rolf mumbled and then he sighed sadly. "No. Never. Strange, and not so strange. Like this winter, I think."

"What do you mean?" Mapaline asked.

Rolf squinted at her, weighing his words. "There are dangers about that have not been here before. Don't you think?"

"Well, yes, I suppose so. It's been very cold."

"And Nettle said she saw a wolf the other day," Red squeaked. "Down in the gorge. She said it was red. 'Like blood.'"

"Nettle talks too much," Aker scoffed.

"Perhaps, perhaps," Rolf grumbled. "Still, there are unusual things about this winter. Unexpected things. At least they are unexpected by you, I think."

Mapaline and the other children stared at him for a moment, trying to work out what seemed to them a riddle of some sort, though they couldn't quite find the turn of it. Finally, Mapaline gave up and asked, "Will you walk us home, Rolf?"

"You are done looking for caves?"

"Well, I . . . With the wolverines . . ."

"We were headed home to tell our father," Aker said. "The men will probably want to form a hunting party to track the beasts down."

Rolf grumbled again and then smiled. He was always forgetting about his smile and that it was not a nice thing to the treeborn. This time it was even more frightful, for blood was on all their minds, and there was some about his jowls as well. Both Aker and Red backed away.

"Sorry," Rolf said. "I didn't mean to frighten you. I only meant . . . well, you have no more to fear from those particular wolverines. And, if you'd like, I could show you something nice."

"Did you follow them? Have they left the area?"

"*Mmmmn*, yes," Rolf said. "More or less. They are gone. They won't be coming back."

"You're sure?"

Another smile almost crept to Rolf's mouth, but this time he caught it before his teeth could show. He nodded instead. "Very sure."

And then the children understood.

"All right," Aker said "I think we can brave the cold for a while longer then. What do you think, Mapaline? Red?"

Both the children nodded happily, and then Rolf turned to walk back down the far side of the hill from which he had come. Mapaline walked next to him, her hand buried deep in his warm fur, and after a few steps she realized that her friend was limping. One of his front legs seemed to be injured.

"Rolf, are you hurt?"

"Just a bit," he said.

"How did you get hurt? Did they . . ."

Rolf let a grumbling, gravelly growl rumble out of him and then swung his head to nuzzle at Mapaline's face. His fur and breath were warm on her skin. I would not like to be so close to a bear's mouth and

Mapaline

I'm sure you wouldn't either, but with Mapaline and Rolf, it was different.

"Don't ask how," Rolf whispered.

Mapaline hated that answer.

Rolf led them on for several more minutes, down through the trees and through a part of the woods in which no trails ran. There were rocks to climb and fallen limbs to duck under and even a shallow, icy stream to slide across. Just about the time that Red began contemplating another whine, Rolf led them up to an overhang of rock that stood out from the hard ground. A trickle of the stream they had passed had been diverted last autumn to run over the stone and had caused the dirt beneath to cave away down the hillside. Now a thin sheet of ice hung from the edge of the rock. Behind it was a hollow space large enough for all three children to squeeze inside.

In a moment they felt almost warm huddled there together. The sun broke through the clouds just then and the wall of ice scattered the light into a million tiny rainbows across the snow and stone and even across Mapaline and her brothers.

"Look!" Red cried. He pointed, smiling, at Mapaline. "You've got colors on your head!"

They all laughed.

Rolf, unfortunately, was too large to fit within the cave, but he, too, smiled at the rainbows dancing through the woods.

"Do you like it?" he asked, though I'm sure he knew that they did. Sometimes it's just nice to hear it said.

"It's wonderful, Rolf!" Mapaline giggled. "Thank you! How did you find it?"

Rolf stuck his nose inside the cave as far as he could, until just one eye was able to see his little treeborn friends. Then, if you can believe it, he winked. At least that's what it looked like to Mapaline.

"I know, I know," she said. "Don't ask how!"

Dear Journal,

There were wolverines in the woods today and Rolf saved us! Well, we didn't actually see them, but they were nearby and i think Rolf killed them. i've never had a friend who could protect me from wolverines before. i've never had a friend like Rolf at all.

Do you know that i've not even thought to ask him where he lived before coming here? i wonder where he came from. i'll have to ask him, though i think i know what he'll say. But even if he won't tell me and wants to keep his mysteries to himself, i'm very glad he's here. i think . . . Don't tell Nettle or Briar, but i think that i've never had a friend i've loved so much as Rolf.

Mapaline

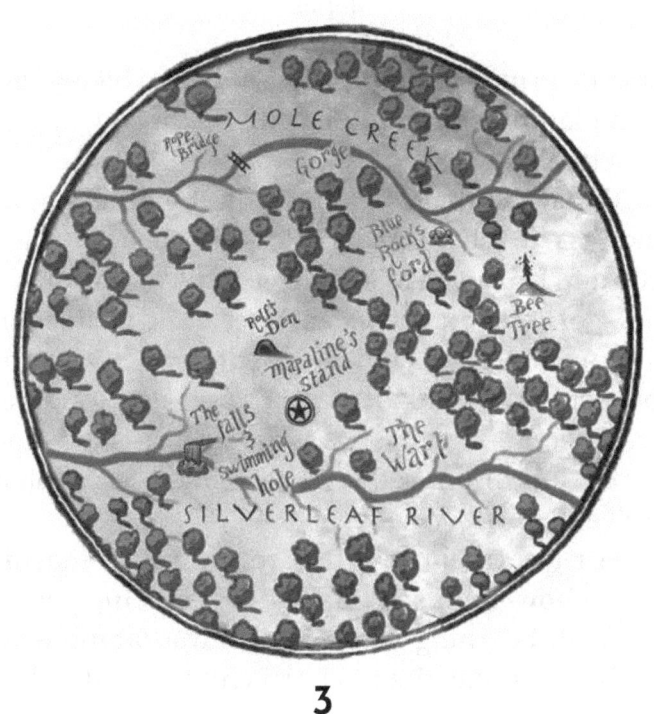

3

Thatch's Blunder

Y OU MAY BE thinking at this point that I've forgotten to mention something very important. Something that you probably think about each and every day, especially in the winter time. Something, in fact, that you may be doing right now.

I'm talking, as you've probably guessed, about school, and you may have wondered why Mapaline spends so much time playing games and hiking about and planning celebrations and no time at all going to school.

I'm afraid that Mapaline and the other sprouts didn't go to school. At all. At least, not like the schools you and I are used to. When we think of learning, we think of desks and pencils and tests and whiteboards and teachers who make us write neatly and spell properly. We think of school buses and loud bells and recess—which is always too short—and report cards and bright red lines crossing out problems we've done incorrectly.

For the treeborn children, however, learning was—how can I say this without making you feel too bad? Learning was . . . well, it was far more *fun*.

For example, the treeborn children didn't learn about animals and plants from a book. They might learn these things from Ever Fir, who would lead some of them out in the fall to search for mushrooms and teach them which were poisonous and which were safe to eat. Or from Mapaline's father, who would explain how deer live and mate and eat, all in the midst of a hunt where they would also learn—if they were successful—about the insides of that deer and which parts were good for food.

The treeborn children didn't learn about history from a book either. At least, not *only* from a book. They might learn about the history of their stand from old Caddo Maple, who would tell them stories every chance he got. They might learn about distant dwarves and giants from the few old books they did have, but then hear all about them afresh around a campfire, listening to tales that had been passed down to their roots from generations past.

The treeborn children didn't learn about art from . . . You get the idea. Sprouts like Mapaline and her friends never went to school, and, at the same time, it was as if they went to school every single day. If the roots took their jobs seriously, as they most often did, by the time a sprout grew up he could read and write and do sums and tell you about a thousand different things that he'd never had a test on in his life.

So you will not be surprised to find Mapaline, notebook and ink and quill in hand, climbing down her tree in the late winter to do some chores . . . *and* some morning mathematics. She didn't waste any time. Though spring was just around the corner, the air was still bitterly cold and she was sick to death of the snow and ice and frost. At the base of her maple tree was a small square door in the earth and she quickly undid the latch and climbed down inside.

It was a bit warmer here. At least there was no wind. A few paces down a tunnel, with the thick roots of her hometree growing all around her, and she came to a sort of cellar carved into the earth and lined with thin planks of cedar. Dried grass covered the ground, and in the dim light she could make out a whole host of boxes and jars and baskets organized neatly along the walls with dried strings of onions and herbs hanging from the ceiling.

This was one of two underground rooms that the treeborn used to store food for the winter. A second was beneath one of the fir trees. Mapaline lit a lamp and raced back up the tunnel to shut the door on the cold day outside. Then it was time to get to work.

Each week the treeborn would check and count their supplies. This gave the sprouts a good opportunity to practice their writing and their sums and, even more importantly, kept the stand from running out of food before spring.

Do you like math? Mapaline did not (learning is not always fun, even for the treeborn). As a matter of fact, right this very instant she could think of at least a hundred and one things she would rather be doing than math. But it had to be done and it had to be done well or the whole stand would suffer. So she began.

Her notebook was soon full of labels and numbers. There was a column for canned vegetables like squash and beets and cucumbers. There was a column for boxes of dried fruit like strawberries and apples and cherries. Columns for bags of grain and bags of nuts and bags of beans. Columns for roots and herbs and . . . on and on it went. Some items, like the canned peppers, Mapaline very much wished would run out so she would not have to eat them anymore. Other items, like the jars of maple syrup, she very much wished to see more of. But she didn't really spend much time thinking about either because there were always more items to count.

Finally, after what seemed like hours, she found herself at the back of the room, sitting in the glow of the lamp, checking her work to be sure it was all done correctly. When she was confident that all her adding and subtracting was accurate, she compared her notes to those from the week before, when Thatch Birch had been assigned the task.

That's when she found them.

Mistakes. Dreadful mistakes. So dreadful, in fact, that Mapaline went back to the beginning of her work and counted the supplies again, from start to finish, just to be sure her own figures were correct. They were, and that meant . . .

Oh dear.

Now she flipped back to the week before last and found that Thatch had done the count for that week as well *and* the week before that. Three weeks in a row, and somewhere in all that scribbling—Thatch's handwriting was thin and tended to wander about the page—mistakes had been made and had turned into further mistakes, which had turned into so many mistakes that they couldn't even be separated from the parts that had been done correctly.

Mapaline saw all this in a few moments' time and covered her mouth with a shaking hand. What could be done? Ideas—crazy ideas—came suddenly running through her head, but each one involved food that they no longer had or that they wouldn't be able to get again until spring or summer. Given time, she could rework Thatch's errors and set the notebook right again, but there was no setting right the stores in the cellar.

Can you remember the last math quiz you took? Perhaps it was multiplication or fractions or making measurements. Did it make you nervous to be taking such a test, to know that, if you accidentally put this number *here* instead of *there*, where it was supposed to go, your teacher would take a big red marker and strike it out? Then maybe, if you'd gotten too many of these red marks, you'd have a frowny face sticker at the top of your page and have to do it over again.

Now imagine that by placing those few numbers in the wrong spots it meant that your family and friends would think you all had more food stored away than you actually did. And imagine that, thinking this, they ate more food and faster than they otherwise would have. And then imagine that, after all that eating, someone discovered your mistake and instead of a red marker slashing out your answer, you found there would not be enough food to last everyone the rest of the winter. Not enough potatoes, not enough flour, not enough canned fruits and vegetables.

These are exactly the kinds of mistakes that Mapaline had discovered. And now she had to go and tell everyone about it.

Somehow the wind felt even colder when she came out of the cellar.

Papa Maple sat at the table in their little living room and looked over the notebook. For the first time in her life, Mapaline hoped that he would find that she had been mistaken. Maybe it was her sums that were wrong and not Thatch's after all and then . . .

But no. Her father's face grew graver and graver and then he stood slowly, said, "Well done, Mapaline," and went to get Green Fir and Moose Birch. After they had looked over the notes again and gone down to the cellar to check for themselves, their faces grew just as grave as Papa's. They asked Mapaline a few questions and thanked her for doing such a good job on her work and discovering the error.

Then they sent for Thatch.

Poor Thatch. It was one thing to be summoned by his father, Moose, and quite another to have to come before Papa and Green Fir as well. Mapaline and her mother were the only others in the room when Thatch came through the door, and they could see by his face, which was birch tree white even under the best of circumstances, that he knew something serious had happened. Something very serious, indeed.

Papa Maple, in his slow, quiet way, explained the errors that had been found in Thatch's sums. All the while Moose sat with his head down and Green was looking very stern, as only a treeborn with sharp, green needles for hair can look, and Thatch looked more and more miserable with every detail given. Then they asked him a few questions and he answered as best he could and then he started to cry.

For a moment no one said anything further. The only sound was the snap and crackle of the fire in the hearth and the sobbing and sniffling of the little treeborn at the table. Mapaline found that she wanted very much to go over and give Thatch a great big hug but felt that it probably wouldn't be appropriate, and the three roots seemed caught between feeling bad for the boy and trying to think what the stand would need to do to make it through the rest of the winter.

Mapaline

It was one of those awkward moments that happen sometimes, when *something* needs to be said or done but no one seems to know exactly what it is or exactly who should say or do it.

You will not be surprised to find that it was Mama Maple who came to the rescue.

"Now that's enough of that," she said kindly and put a hand on Thatch's back as she reached across the table for the jar of honey. Soon she had six wooden mugs filled with tea and spoonfuls of honey swirling about in them (Mapaline was sure she saw Mama put an extra spoonful in Thatch's cup), and then she stood back and held her own mug right up under her nose to breathe in the smell. "Enough crying from sprouts and enough sulking and worrying from roots. Now's the time to think what's to be done."

Aren't mothers wonderful?

Papa Maple sat up straight and smiled at his wife. "Very well, Mama Maple. You're right."

"It was an honest mistake, Thatch," said Moose. "It's really as much my fault as anyone's for not checking your work more often. It's a job for two or three pairs of eyes, not just one."

"We'll be all right," said Green, and though still deep and stern, there was kindness in the tone. "There's still the food in the other cellar. And we have emergency supplies across the Silverleaf. They'll be difficult to dig out in this cold, but it can be done."

"And we can double the traps downstream," said Papa Maple. "A few more hunts . . . We will have to be careful. No more feasts and less vegetables in the stew. But we'll make it through to spring even if we are lighter around the middle when we get there."

Finally, after all the serious, somber faces, a few smiles broke through.

Then Thatch did something truly admirable. He'd had his cry. He'd said his apologies. Now he tried to set things right.

"Father, I can set the traps," he said. "I've done it with you and Ever a dozen times. Just last week we walked along the lines and I know where some extra snares can be set. I can do it today . . . right now . . . and be back by nightfall."

Moose and Green and Papa Maple all looked at one another with raised eyebrows and squinty, thoughtful faces.

"I don't know, Thatch," Moose said. "It certainly would be good to get them set as quickly as possible . . ."

"But it's not really a one-person job," Papa said. "I don't think—"

"I'll go with him," Mapaline said. "And I'll bet Rolf will come too, so we won't be by ourselves."

For a moment—a very long moment—everyone in the room paused and stared at Mapaline.

Then Papa said, "Yes. Rolf . . ."

And Green said, "Um, well . . ."

And Moose and Thatch both looked at each other with nervous expressions on their faces.

"What's the matter?" Mapaline asked. "You're not still scared of Rolf, are you?"

"No, not scared, just . . ."

"Um, well . . ."

"Perhaps it would be best if . . ."

"Oh, stop," said Mama Maple, and though her voice was a bit trembly, she looked them all in the eye and said, "If that bear was going to eat us, he'd have done so at the Short Day festival. You rode on his back, Thatch, and you helped him move the deer he brought for the feast, Green. He's very . . . safe. I'm sure of it. The children will be fine, and we need the traps to be set, don't we? Thatch is perfectly capable and Mapaline and . . . and Rolf will help him."

The three other roots scowled a bit and Thatch gave a nervous chuckle and a half smile.

But Mapaline beamed.

THERE WAS NO time to lose. Thatch left immediately to gather the supplies they would need. Mapaline climbed up to her little room and dressed for a long day outside: heavy squirrel-skin jacket, mouse boots and mouse mittens, knit cap with a downy lining. Over it all she draped a long, thick cape to bundle everything together in a pinch. The clothing was heavy and made movement slow and more difficult, but once she had gone back outside, she was glad for the warmth. The sky was a clear, icy blue and the frigid wind tried to steal her breath away.

Down the hillside she went, in the opposite direction of the river, as fast as her heavy clothes would let her. Thankfully, Rolf was at home sleeping in his den. It took some work to wake him, but after some shouting and what poking she could manage from the outside, he was awake enough to hear her story.

Thatch's Blunder

Naturally he agreed to help, and as his thick winter coat could never be taken off, they didn't have to waste any time putting it on: they were off immediately to meet with Thatch.

It was a two-hour walk to the trapline. Rolf slung a bag of heavy metal traps across his back and the two treeborn carried their share of stakes and bait and coiled rope. They went across the frozen Silverleaf and up the ridge on the far side, then down again into the deeper woods to the south.

"How much farther?" Mapaline asked after a long while. She was not feeling quite as excited about the adventure now as she had been at the start. If you have ever done a good bit of hard walking in the winter, especially if you are bundled up as thoroughly as Mapaline was, you know that eventually you begin to feel very hot and sweaty around the middle and very cold everywhere else.

"Not far," Thatch said. "Actually, there's the first trap right there." He pointed. Between two large oak trees were some bushes on a gentle slope.

Rolf stopped and stared. He squinted his eyes. Then he blinked and opened them wide.

"Where?" he said.

"Right there. See the rabbit trail cutting through those bushes?"

"Yes."

"See the open space at the bottom, between the trees?"

"Yes."

"Now look up."

Rolf looked up. High above, one of the oaks threw a

heavy limb out across the clearing, and stretched from this branch to the ground was the thinnest of lines. A bright red flag was tied onto it a few feet from the top.

"The flag warns other treeborn who might pass this way that there's a snare set here. Otherwise, someone might stumble into it by accident."

"Didn't you know?" Mapaline asked.

Rolf shook his head. "No. I've never set a trapline before. How would I know?"

"Well, I just thought . . . You always seem to . . . I just . . ." Mapaline looked at him and thought how mysterious he could be sometimes and then said, "Never mind."

"So what do we do now?" Rolf asked.

Thatch shifted the pack on his shoulders and pointed. "There's a line of snares and traps set from here back through the woods to the southwest. Caddo was out to check them early this morning so there's no sense going over them again. We'll walk a while and set a new series to the southeast."

And so they did. Mapaline had only set a trapline two or three times before, so Thatch explained what he was doing for each one and why he chose this spot over that one and where the bait was to be placed. Sometimes it would be a steel-jawed trap with sharp teeth and a strong spring and sometimes it was one of various sorts of snares that Thatch would contrive from branches and ropes. Each time a red flag would be attached somewhere overhead.

By the time six or seven had been set, the sun was coursing downward, and the temperature with it.

"One more and we'll be done," Thatch said. "You

Thatch's Blunder

can stay here for this one. I'll be quick so we can get home."

The ground they had come to was in a narrow gully and the far end was strewn with piles of stones and boulders. Thatch grabbed the last steel trap and started climbing atop the nearest pile, looking for possible dens to target.

"Rolf," Mapaline said after a moment. She leaned into him and buried her hands deep in his fur. "Does it bother you to help set the traps?"

"Bother me?" He craned his neck to look down at her.

"Yes. I mean . . . well, the traps are set for animals. Not like you, of course, but animals still. And you're an animal."

"Am I?" he said, and then, "Of course I am. But why should it bother me?"

"We need them for their pelts and meat and such. But I just thought you might not like helping. Or that it would bother you somehow."

"I eat animals."

"Yes, I know, but . . . never mind."

Sometimes Rolf could be very difficult.

Suddenly there was a loud *snap* and a cry and a thump from above them in the rocks.

"Thatch?" Mapaline called. "Thatch, are you all right?"

"Help!" The cry sounded like it was coming from far away. "Help!"

"Go on, Mapaline," Rolf said. "I'm coming."

The boulders were tumbled all together as if they were great, lumpy marbles poured from a giant bag.

Mapaline found a foothold on the first and was soon atop it, leaping from here to there to get higher up the pile. Rolf circled off to the left looking for a way to follow her, but the stones were unsteady and the way dangerous for a bear his size.

"Help! I'm in here!"

The call was closer this time. Mapaline skirted another huge slab of stone and found a little snow-covered track that led among a few smaller roundish ones. Then she stopped. On her right was an opening in the ground, the space between several rocks that were braced against one another, and its mouth was tucked in between things so you could almost stumble into it unawares. From the darkness of the hole Thatch's voice echoed out.

"Help!"

"I'm here! Where are you?"

"Down in this hole. I've . . . I've got the trap sprung on my own leg and I'm wedged in here tight. Can you see me?"

Mapaline peered in. It was very dark, but from somewhere farther down light was leaking in through other seams between the rocks. She squinted and could just make out the shape of Thatch's head and shoulders. He was looking up at her and the light glinted off his eyes.

"I see you! Are you hurt?"

"Um . . . yes," he said, and then she could hear it in his voice, a strain like he was holding back tears and trying to be brave. "Yes, my leg is hurt pretty bad, I think. I was trying to set the trap and then slipped right into it. Then I fell down here and . . . I'm pretty stuck."

Mapaline straightened up and looked for Rolf. He was still down on the level ground behind her.

"Rolf, he's fallen in a hole! Can you come up and help?"

Rolf looked up at her and then took a tentative step over two boulders and onto a third, but the stone slid beneath his weight and his paw twisted and slammed awkwardly into another rock. He tried again and got a few feet farther, but the whole pile seemed ready to shift and tumble at any moment and he was forced to stop again.

"Oh dear," Mapaline whispered. She turned back to Thatch. "Thatch, Rolf can't climb up here. He's too big."

"All right, well . . ."

She could see the sprout shifting and reaching his arms up as high as they would go, trying to find some purchase on a stone to pull himself up. But then he cried out in pain and slumped back down again. It was no good.

"Should I run back to the stand for help?" Mapaline asked, but knew just as she said it that she couldn't. The sun was nearly set and what had been a bitterly cold day was promising to be an absolutely frigid night. It was a good two-hour hike back to the stand, even going as fast as she could possibly go, and then two hours back—far too long for Thatch to be outside, pressed against hard, cold stones that were even now sucking the warmth out of him. And there was no way to build him a fire or even cover him with her cape.

"Oh dear," she said again to herself. "Thatch?" This time he didn't answer.

"What's going on up there?" Rolf called.

Mapaline

"He's stuck and . . ." Mapaline looked around. There were no branches nearby and nothing to dig with, even if the rocks and earth hadn't been frozen solid. But Thatch's pack lay nearby and she still had her own.

Rope.

They had plenty of rope and some of it was quite strong. Mapaline grabbed what was left in Thatch's bag and began climbing back down to Rolf, thinking hard. By the time she reached him she had a plan. Sort of. At least it seemed like *most* of a plan, and she was hoping the rest would fill in as she went along.

"Rolf, I think I can reach him with these ropes," she said and then began tying two lengths together with a strong knot. "If you hold one end, I can climb down into the hole and wrap the other around Thatch's arms. Then . . . do you think you can pull us out?"

"Yes," Rolf said, but he was looking at Mapaline with a strange expression on his face. It is hard to describe exactly what he looked like because a bear's face is so different from yours or mine. It was not fear but worry, maybe, stretching at his eyes and spreading out his ears. But there was something else. Surprise, perhaps. Or wonder. Like he was seeing a part of Mapaline that he hadn't seen before.

"Right," Mapaline said, and then she turned to look back up into the rocks. "I think I can fit down inside easily enough. I'm much smaller than Thatch, and then . . . Rolf, why are you looking at me like that?"

"Hmmm?" he said, and then shook his head. "Nothing at all, Mapaline. Go ahead. Just shout when you're ready for me to pull."

He bent his head down low and took the end of

the rope between his fierce jaws. Then he wrapped the line around one of his paws several times as an anchor.

Mapaline dashed back up as fast as she could go, dragging the other end of the rope with her and being careful not to go stumbling into Thatch's hole before she was ready. It was really getting dark now and clouds were moving in. No moonlight. No starlight. In a few moments she wouldn't be able to see a thing, and then this would be *really* difficult. She made it past the last stone and found the opening, which now appeared even darker and deeper than it had twenty minutes ago.

"Thatch!" she called down. "Thatch, I'm coming down to get you!"

And then . . . well, then she stopped. Up until this point, Mapaline had been focused on the plan. Now she was faced with the hole and the fact that *she* had to climb down into it. Really, it was just about the last thing she wanted to do at the moment. She would have chosen a dozen mathematics assignments before clambering down a slick, cold shaft with nothing but a thin snare line, hoping that the knots would hold and that Rolf could really pull them out and knowing that if they didn't or he couldn't, there was no one else around to save her and . . .

In any other circumstance, I believe that Mapaline would have been too frightened to continue. But sometimes, when there truly is no other choice, it is amazing what we can do.

Mapaline

So down she went. The climb was really not that difficult as the sides were not smooth but made up of all sorts of rock and stone jumbled tightly together. There were plenty of handholds, and though it was slick, she managed to reach Thatch in just a couple minutes.

"Thatch?" she said softly. She could only see the outlines of his face below her; the rest of his body was lost to the gloom farther down.

"Hello, Mapaline," he said, and his voice sounded very tired. "You shouldn't be down here. You'll get stuck too."

"We're going to be just fine," she said. "Here. Can you lean forward? I'll put this rope around you."

Thatch leaned forward as much as he could and Mapaline bent down to wrap the rope around his back and under his arms. Then she tied a slip knot—"You must know your knots," her father always said when she complained of the practice—and cinched it up tight. She had planned, at this point, to hold on to the rope and let Rolf pull them both out, but thought now that she could climb out herself rather easily.

She scrambled up a few feet and then shouted, "Rolf! Rolf! Pull him up, Rolf!"

There was a moment's pause and then the line went taut and began to inch upward. Thatch winced and groaned as his body shifted and all those muscles, still and cold for so long, discovered just how stiff they had become. But he was more alert now and began using his arms to help the ascent. Mapaline climbed too, staying just above him and helping whenever the rope got stuck on something or Thatch slipped and spun around.

Then they were at the top. Mapaline climbed out and helped Thatch over the edge and onto his back. It was so dark now that she couldn't see anything.

"Can you walk?"

Thatch moaned. "I don't think so. Maybe a little. The trap's still on my leg, but I don't think we should take it off now; it may be helping to stop the bleeding. My other leg is bruised up pretty good as well, but I don't think it's broken."

"Come on. I'll help you."

It took all Mapaline's strength to help Thatch to his feet—or *foot*—and down through the rocks back to Rolf. The bear was waiting anxiously for them and took a moment to sniff Thatch all over, snuffling at his injuries and breathing warm, bear breath into his face. Thatch seemed to revive at this and was able to grab hold of Rolf's fur and climb up onto his back. Mapaline threw her cape over him, and the three set off for home.

THERE ARE SOME days—and if you haven't had one yet, I'm afraid that someday you certainly will—that seem set on delivering trouble after trouble. From the moment you wake up, the world seems against you and it seems to keep on against you through lunchtime and nap time and the afternoon all the way until you can finally fall into bed, very glad that you'll get a fresh start the next morning.

Today had been that sort of day for Mapaline. By the time they had reached the stand and explained the day's events to all the roots and Thatch was bandaged up and in his hometree sleeping soundly, she was more than ready for bed. But just now, standing at the foot of her own tree, she wasn't at all sure she had the energy to climb to her room.

"Thank you, Rolf," she said, but it was really more of a mumble, for she was already half asleep.

He nuzzled her face with his warm snout and helped boost her the first few feet upwards. After she had climbed a few more, he called to her and she looked back down. All she could see of him was a half shape reflecting the lamplight from one of the windows above their heads.

"I was very proud of you today," he said.

"You did all the hard work, Rolf. Without you, I never would have been able to get Thatch out of that hole."

"I didn't say I was proud of your strength, Mapaline. I'm proud of *you*. For volunteering to go with Thatch in the first place and for being brave and tough till the end. I think . . . I think you'll do just fine."

"Just fine at what, Rolf?"

He blinked a couple times and looked down suddenly at his feet. "Oh, just at everything, Mapaline. At everything that comes."

Mapaline didn't understand but was too tired, far too tired, to talk about it anymore. "Anyway, I don't feel very brave or tough right now."

"Neither do I. Good night, Mapaline."

"Good night, Rolf."

He turned, but then, despite her drooping eyelids and cold fingers, Mapaline called after him one more time. "Rolf? Do you think winter is almost over? It seems like spring will never come."

"Spring always comes, Mapaline. Sooner or later, it always comes."

"Good night, Rolf."

"Good night."

Dear Journal,

i'm writing this morning because i was so tired last night that i forgot something important. During our long walk to lay the trapline, i finally got up the courage to ask Rolf the question i've been meaning to for so long. Why was i so nervous? i don't know, but i was. So i asked him where he came from, and do you know what he said? He hemmed and hawed as usual, but eventually he told me that he'd come from over the mountains. The Splintered Mountains! That's farther than i can even imagine!

i asked him how long he'd lived there and he said forty or fifty years. i don't think normal bears even live that long, but i'm going to check with Papa tomorrow to be sure. As you might guess, Rolf grumbled and mumbled in his usual way and then changed the subject before i could ask more. And then everything happened with Thatch and i never got back to it. But isn't that strange?

Mapaline

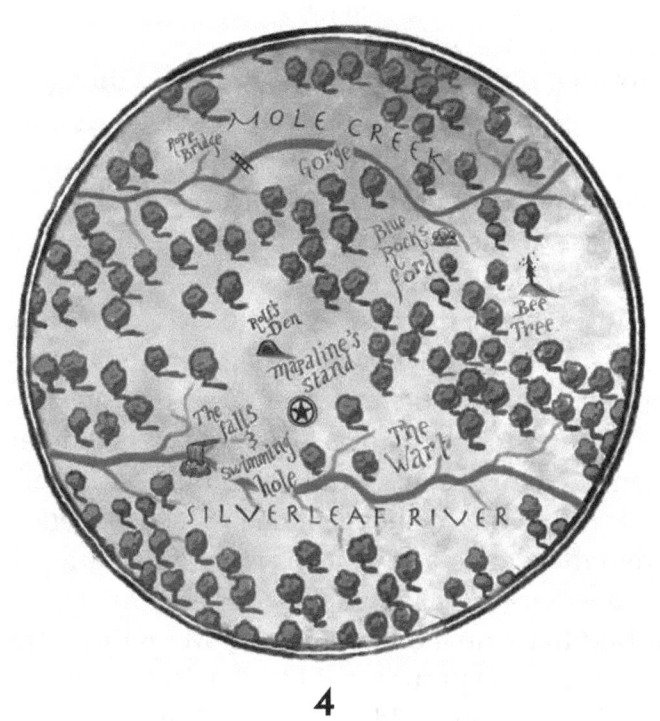

4

Danger at Mole Creek

AND SPRING DOES come, eventually. One morning you wake up and the air is not quite so biting and the blue of the sky has changed from pale and icy to rich and warm. Then the next morning is the same, and the next, and though you continue to get some unwelcomely bitter days thrown in, you know that the march of the seasons has not been checked and spring is drawing near.

It was at this time of year that the treeborn children began to look for risers.

Risers were the first sign of life to emerge from winter's sleep; the first spark of green and purple to sprout, even from beneath the snow, and reach for the warming sun. By the time the snow was completely gone, riser blossoms would cover the surrounding hillsides in broad sheets of deep violet, as different from the blankets of white as warmth is from cold.

But there was always a *first* riser, and over the years it had become a contest within Mapaline's stand to see which sprout would find it. Rules had developed—how you could prove you'd found the first and whether or not you should pick it—and an official ceremony of sorts at which the eldest member of the stand would award a prize to whoever had found this first sign of spring. Sometimes it was a length of brightly colored ribbon purchased from the traveling merchants. Sometimes a pinch of gold dust or a small gemstone recovered from the river downstream. The prize itself didn't really matter. What mattered was finding the *first*. What mattered was being able to officially declare that the winter was over and warmer days were to come.

At least, that was the idea. Sometimes, however, things got a little out of hand.

Nettle Fir had found the first riser for three years in a row and with each successive victory had become more impressed with her own achievement. All the past year, in fact, it seemed that every time she and her friends passed a patch of risers growing in their stand or the surrounding hills, she had made a not-so-subtle reference to the springtime contest.

"Oh, look! These risers are just like the ones I found last spring."

"This is just the sort of place where risers love to grow. I know lots about risers. That's how I find them so quickly."

"Those are lovely risers! And look! They match the ribbon I chose for my hair today. I won it in the riser contest, you know."

As you can imagine, this sort of thing became more and more grating on the nerves of her friends. It became harder and harder to keep the snide remarks that came into their heads from spilling out of their mouths. They began to avoid risers whenever Nettle was around, and on more than one occasion Mapaline found herself stomping on clumps of the purple blossoms out of spite and annoyance.

This was how it came to be that, on a morning in late winter when the sun was up and shining and the snow was beginning to turn to slush and fall heavily from the trees, Mapaline and Red and Briar Maple began to conspire against their friend.

"She's out looking already," Mapaline said with a groan.

They were gathered up in Mapaline's room, the

girls sitting on her bed and Red peering out the wavy glass of the window into the sun.

"She's been looking for days," said Briar, who, being a maple, looked much like Mapaline in skin and build, though she was a bit taller. "For days! I even heard that she convinced Rollwater to do her morning chores so she could begin her search earlier than anyone else."

"My brother never does *my* chores," Mapaline said and flung a pillow at Red.

Red ignored her and there was a silent, brooding pause before he said what everyone was thinking. "I don't think I can stand it if she wins again this year. I'd rather anyone win than her."

Mapaline and Briar mumbled their agreement, and then there was another somber moment when no one spoke. Brows became furrowed. Faces scowled and pinched in concentration. They were . . . What's the word? Scheming. Brainstorming. Searching desperately for a way to keep the best riser finder in the stand from finding the first riser of the season . . . again.

I'm afraid that some of the ideas that wandered through their conversation were not particularly kind or honest. Red briefly considered tying Nettle up in her bedroom until the contest was over, which was not at all practical and certainly not nice, though the thought did make him chuckle. Briar found herself hoping that her friend would get sick or maybe sprain an ankle and be unable to go out for a week or so. Mapaline contemplated starting rumors of "riser sightings" that might get Nettle to run off looking for flowers that weren't there.

As I said, these were not terribly nice thoughts, and to be fair, none of them seriously considered doing such underhanded things. Nettle was still their friend, after all, and they didn't really want her to be hurt or lied to. They just didn't want her to win. The problem facing them was this: Nettle truly *was* very good at searching for risers. She had sharp eyes and a sharp nose—she claimed, repeatedly, to have "smelled them before I even saw them"—and had spent many lazy afternoons talking to the older roots about plants and flowers and how they grew and what conditions favored them and so on. She was, quite simply, better at the game than everyone else, and her past success had only encouraged her to get better.

So, other than the devious possibilities, Mapaline, Red, and Briar could think of nothing to do to prevent Nettle from winning.

Until . . .

"Wait!" said Mapaline. "Why didn't I think of this before? I'll ask Rolf. He must know plenty about risers and where they're most likely to grow. He could help us."

Red turned around and scratched at his bald head; it always itched most just before the hair began to bud. "Rolf knows lots about risers?"

"Well," Mapaline said, and suddenly it didn't seem as obvious as when the thought first struck her. "Well, he's an animal and . . . animals have a sense for that sort of thing."

"They do?" Briar asked.

"Sure. They live out in the woods their whole lives and . . ."

"So do we."

"Yes, but . . . well, Rolf is different." Mapaline paused. "He's a very wise bear and I just feel like he probably . . . knows about such things."

Briar and Red looked at each other.

"Do either of you have any better ideas?"

"Not really," said Briar.

"Not unless we tie her up in her room until the contest is over," said Red, but he was smiling and giggling and not serious. At least, not *very* serious.

"Well then," said Mapaline, "I say we go and ask Rolf. I'm sure he can help."

"Risers?" said Rolf in his deep, mumbly, just-woke-up-from-a-nap voice. "What are risers?"

Mapaline, Red, and Briar had walked down the hill and were gathered outside the entrance to Rolf's den. They had most certainly woken him up, though he denied it, and they had already tried to explain themselves twice before. Bears do not wake up very quickly under the best of circumstances and, to be honest, he was only partly awake even now. What he needed was a bit of patience from these sprouts, but Mapaline and the others were not feeling patient. With every moment that passed, every hour that moved toward spring, the fear grew inside them that Nettle would come charging out of the woods holding a perfect little flower high in the air.

"Yes, Rolf, risers," said Mapaline again. She talked very slowly this time, to try to get him to understand.

"You know, the flowers that always show themselves earliest in the spring. We have a contest and . . ."

"*Bbbrrnnnm*," Rolf mumbled and stretched and came clambering out of his den. The sprouts scooted quickly out of his way and then watched as he awkwardly stretched his legs, one at a time, all while wearing a ridiculous, sleepy grimace on his face. There were times when Rolf was regal and noble and awe-inspiring, like someone out of an ancient tale of heroes. There were other times when . . . well . . . when he was not.

"Yes," he said finally. "I know risers."

"Can you help us find some?" Red asked.

"Why?"

"Because," Mapaline said, "we *want* to win the *contest!*"

Rolf glanced at her sideways and stretched once more, taking his time, before saying, "There's no need for grumpiness, Mapaline. If anyone has a reason to be grumpy, perhaps it's the fellow who's been woken from his sleep to help you all beat your friend at a silly game."

How Rolf knew about Nettle, Mapaline didn't know, but she was coming to expect such things from him. He seemed to know all sorts of things about their stand and those who lived there and, particularly, about Mapaline herself. For a time she had even wondered if he'd somehow gotten hold of her journal. The fact that he couldn't possibly fit into her room ruled this out, but it remained that she had come to expect Rolf to know things long before it seemed he should. Long before she told him. Sometimes before she even knew herself.

She did not like being corrected by him, but was not yet ready to give a real apology and so only said, "Sorry, Rolf" and sulked a moment till he was completely and thoroughly awake.

"*Mmrrrlllmm*," he grumbled again, and then, "I'm not sure I particularly like that you're conspiring against Nettle, but I'll play along for the moment. First, though, before we do any flower *hunting*, I must do some food *finding*. I'm hungry."

Briar laughed. "Mapaline told us you'd say that. I know it's not much, but we brought you something." She revealed a little clay jar of honey and a loaf of freshly baked bread. She placed both on the ground before the bear, along with a few salted fish, and Rolf studied them for a moment. He knew that food was short in the stand, and I think he was nervous that the sprouts had sacrificed their own breakfasts for him.

"Don't worry, Rolf," Mapaline said. "We've all eaten. Besides, remember the wild pig you brought us last week? Think of it as a trade."

Rolf considered this for a moment and then, the decision made, he swallowed the food up with relish.

"Thank you," he said finally, and licked his lips of the last traces of honey. "Better, I suppose, a too-early breakfast than no breakfast at all. Now . . ." Then he rose up on his hind legs to reach his coal-black nose high into the air and sniff the breeze.

When he came back down, he grunted once and said simply, "This way," and off they went, not toward the river, which was generally considered one of the best places to look for early risers, but in the opposite direction, continuing downhill until the land flattened out and the woods grew deeper. It was colder here than it had been up on the treeborn's hill, and the snow was less melted, so the sprouts soon began to wonder where Rolf was leading them. Risers come out, of course, with the warmth of spring, and so it was commonly reasoned that the buds never first appeared in the deep forest where the trees shaded and sheltered the snow but out in the open where the earth could feel the sun.

Yet on Rolf trudged, and every few minutes he would stop and raise himself up again to sniff at the wind. Despite their doubts, Mapaline and the others kept quiet, partly because they trusted their friend and partly because they felt he was still a bit cross at them for waking him so rudely. Sometimes it is best to keep doubts and criticisms to oneself.

They walked for upwards of two hours and then, quite suddenly, the trees thinned and the land fell away down a few short cliffs to a stream far below. Mapaline and the others knew the place at once and wondered again why Rolf had chosen to come this way. The cliffs here were crumbly and dangerous to climb on. Below, the stream, which they all called Mole Creek, dug its way through a narrow gully, carving out a deep, swift channel that could be frightening even during dry times. Now, with melted snow trickling down from where the sun did its warm work, the water rushed by, loud and fast and cold.

Upstream about four miles there was a good crossing, and downstream about half as far was a rope bridge that Mapaline's own father had strung up years ago. It seemed that Rolf had missed them both.

"How will we get across?" Briar asked. "It's another half an hour at least to the bridge."

"And double that up to the ford at Blue Rocks," Red said. "Rolf, you're not lost, are you?"

Mapaline knew better than to suspect that her friend had lost his way. He seemed to always know exactly what he was doing, and by the look on his furry face she suspected that he did now as well. So instead of questioning him, she began to look around. If Rolf had brought them here, to a sheer drop into tumbling whitewater, then *here* is where he meant to bring them. But why?

It was then that Mapaline stepped to the edge of the cliff and saw two things, almost at the same time.

The first was a small patch of brilliant purple flowers growing out from a ledge about halfway down the cliff.

The second was Nettle Fir.

"Oh no," Mapaline said softly, and then Red and Briar were standing beside her, groaning as well. Nettle was below them and off to the right. She had apparently found a way down onto the cliffs and was now inching along ledges and cracks toward the patch of risers. The year's *first* patch of risers.

"We'll never beat her now," Red moaned. "She's going to win again!"

It was certainly true. Nettle had only a few feet to go

before she would be able to reach out and pluck the first riser from the ground and the contest would be over until next year. The way down the cliff where the children stood was very steep and still patchy with melting snow and ice, and there were no obvious branches or vines to help them climb even if they were foolish enough to try it. The game was up, it seemed, and all three of them immediately began to imagine the long year stretched out in front of them filled with Nettle's success and boasting. It was not a pleasant picture.

But then something happened for which there is really no excuse. Two somethings, actually.

The first is that Nettle happened to look up and see them all standing there, and instead of greeting them or asking for help, she immediately recognized the looks of despair on their faces and *smiled*. Not a normal, "How are you?" or "Good to see you" smile, but a very distinct, "Look, I've beat you again!" smile that was really meant to irritate them further than they were already irritated. It was not a nice thing to do and, I'm afraid, came from a place inside Nettle that actually *wanted* to see her friends upset by her success. I know this sounds terrible. We'd all like to believe that such a thing was not possible for a sweet little sprout like Nettle Fir. Just as we'd all like to believe that this same feeling could never be found within our own hearts when it most certainly can.

The second something that happened was that Nettle's smile so infuriated Briar that for the briefest of moments all common sense left her and she simply *had* to beat Nettle to the risers. *Had* to! It was not a very long moment, but it was enough time for her anger to send her sprawling to the ground, twisting around, and over the edge of the cliff on her stomach. This seemed to surprise even Rolf, and no one was able to grab her arm before she was slipping and sliding down the rocks out of their grasp. Halfway down to the risers' ledge she caught hold of a crack with her toes and another with her long, spindly fingers and came to a stop.

"Briar!" cried Mapaline. "What are you doing?"

"You'll fall!" yelled Nettle, and all the boasting was gone from her face in an instant.

For Briar's part, the short descent had shocked the anger and annoyance right out of her. Her front side was all wet with snow and trickling water, her fingers were burning from holding on so tightly to the narrow crevice, and her toes, though they were strong, were slipping bit by bit from their hold on the cliff face. She knew in a flash that climbing down like that had been foolish, but some things cannot be undone. There was no going back and she was in trouble.

"Red, see if you can find a vine or a long branch," Rolf said, and the little sprout went running back into the woods to look.

"Hold on!" yelled Mapaline, but then Briar's toes finally slipped and down she slid again and everyone—even Rolf—was crying out and shouting in alarm. Then her fingers found another hold and her foot a bit of a root sticking out from the broken stone. She had stopped sliding—for the moment.

"Rolf, is there anything you can do?" Mapaline asked.

Rolf kept looking down over the edge, his brows

furrowed, with as worried an expression on his face as you have ever seen from a bear.

"Can't you just . . . just . . . ," Mapaline stammered, but then didn't really know what to suggest. She knew her friend was not particularly "normal"—she had not forgotten the incident with the fires on Short Day—but really, she could think of nothing that even a bear like Rolf could do for her friend. Unless . . .

"I can't fly, if that's what you mean," Rolf said, guessing at her thoughts. "Not *now*, anyway," he seemed to say almost to himself.

This struck Mapaline as a particularly odd thing to say and there seemed a kind of logic in it that she couldn't make sense of. But then Red arrived back, empty-handed, and she forgot all about it.

"I can't find anything!" Red said between gasps for breath. "Is she all right?"

"Yes, but not for long," Mapaline answered. "It's too slippery."

"There!" Rolf said and pointed with a long, curved claw toward Nettle, who was still shimmying in Briar's direction.

They could see now that there was a wide crack in the cliff running diagonally from Nettle's feet toward the ledge where the risers grew. It seemed that she had plenty of purchase on the stone face to move safely as long as she went slowly and tested her steps for ice and snow. In a few moments she would be to the ledge and find herself only a few feet below where Briar was so precariously perched.

A few more steps and she was there.

"Okay, Briar, I'm right below you," she called up. "I'm right here."

"Can you catch her?" Red shouted down, but they could all see that this would be the end of them both. The ledge was not nearly wide enough for Nettle to stand firmly and catch anything, much less Briar, who was the same size as she was.

"No, but I can see better than she can," Nettle called up. "Briar, there's a little place where you can put your right foot, just below the root. Reach down . . . farther . . . there, do you feel it? Good, now reach down and grab hold of the root with your left hand. That's right. Do you have it?"

And so on. From her vantage point she could see the best and driest places that Briar could reach, and even though Briar could not see them herself, Nettle was able to guide her bit-by-anxious-bit down to the ledge.

As you can imagine, there was a great sigh of relief from the top of the cliff.

Now the two girls simply moved back along the crack that had brought Nettle to the ledge in the first place. Well, not "simply." It was still quite a climb, and Briar's hands were shaking from the fear that had just raced through her. It took some time and some coaxing by everyone involved to get her safely to the long roots of a sycamore tree that tangled down the cliff, way off to their right. That's how Nettle had gotten down, and from there it was an easy climb back to the top where Mapaline, Red, and Rolf were waiting.

After a few minutes all the hugging and crying and shaking were past and everyone was back to smiling and laughing. What had been very frightening was turning quickly into a good story.

"But why did you do it, Briar?" asked Nettle. "Did you really want to win so badly? It's just a silly game."

There was a pause for a moment. Mapaline, Red, and Briar looked at each other, and then at the ground and then up at the trees above them. They all knew what they *wanted* to say, but you know how it is. Sometimes it's difficult to find words that are both true and kind at the same time.

Finally, Rolf said, "*Is* it just a silly game, Nettle?"

"Well, yes. It's just a fun game we play; it's for everyone to enjoy no matter who wins. I don't see why she would —" And then Rolf raised his eyebrows and she stopped and looked around at the others.

"Oh," she said. "I suppose . . . maybe I haven't made it much fun for the rest of you, have I?"

"You've been terrible," said Mapaline.

"Nauseating," said Briar.

"I wanted to tie you up," said Red, and they all laughed. Then Red stood up and walked back over to the edge of the cliff. "Still, I *would* like to win. I think I can still . . ."

"Too late," Rolf said. "I'm afraid this year's contest has already been won."

"By who?" Mapaline asked. "Nettle, you didn't manage to grab a riser in the middle of all that, did you?"

"No, no," Rolf said in his best deep and beary grumble. "Not Nettle."

"Then who?"

"*Hmmrrmm*," Rolf mumbled and then he did something very unexpected. Something Mapaline had never seen him do before. He rolled right over onto his back and raised his forepaws high in the air. And then, while making a noise that could only be described as laughter, though it sounded wilder and more ferocious than most laughs you or I have heard, he produced a single purple riser between the claws of his right paw.

The sprouts all gaped.

"How . . . ," Mapaline began, but Rolf ignored her. Instead, he laughed and laughed and laughed, and very soon the children were climbing atop his belly and laughing too.

Dear Journal,

Rolf said something very strange today that i've been thinking about ever since. in all the excitement with Nettle and Briar, he said, "i can't fly . . . not now, anyway." Doesn't that mean that he could fly at some point? But how can that be possible? Bears don't fly. Even talking bears, as far as i know.

But i suppose i don't really know that much about talking bears, do i? Everything i've learned about Rolf so far has been odd and odder still, and if he wasn't such a dear, dear friend, i think i would be frightened of him. i don't like pestering him with questions and he doesn't seem to like answering them. Still, sometimes i think—i really think—that there's more he wants to tell me, but doesn't.

Anyway, this strange year is all the stranger for him being around. And i wouldn't trade it for anything.

                                        Mapaline

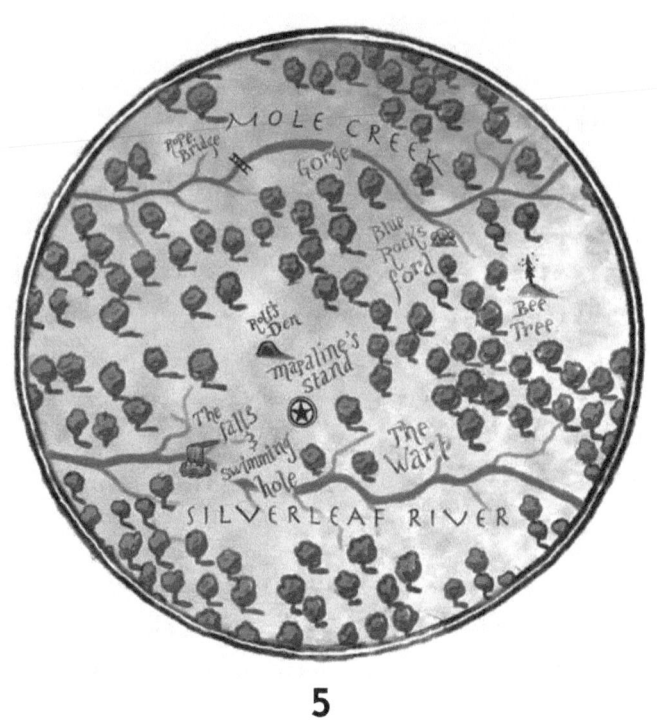

5

A Peculiar Visitor

Soon it was not just risers showing their faces to the sun. New growth began to explode from every tree and bush and flower and tuft of ground and, like every spring, the trees in Mapaline's stand had to be pruned. Not the wild ones, of course. Just the hometrees. If you have never seen a tree pruned, it might seem like an odd thing. The treeborn take their little saws and clippers and snip off whole piles of new branches. When they are done, the ground beneath their trees is littered with so many clippings that you would think a storm had come through and done great damage.

In fact, it was not harmful to the trees at all. It helped keep them healthy and shapely and strong.

This was the chore that had kept Mapaline busy all morning. She was up high, perched in the very tippy-top branches of her maple tree, and had just finished with the shoots coming off of a particularly large limb far below. She was tired—who wouldn't be after climbing and trimming since just after dawn —but it was a very happy and contented tired. The sun was hot, but the gentle breeze was cool, and for a treeborn there are few places as comfortable and peaceful as being among the branches of their own hometree. It's like . . . like . . . well, it's like this: We have all been hugged by friends and distant relatives, and this is nice in its own way. But a hug, a *real* hug from someone you love very much, is another thing entirely, isn't it?

That's what it was like for Mapaline working in her tree. A great big leafy hug from someone she loved very much.

Isn't that wonderful?

Mapaline was even more hesitant than usual to leave the treetop today. The high perch was not only a lovely place to sway in the spring air. It was also a perfect perch from which to watch for the merchant caravan.

Every spring, about this time, a little wagon train

would roll along the rough paths through the Wilderness from stand to stand selling things that most treeborn communities could not make on their own. Things like tools and glass and arrowheads and special silky fabrics; foods from far away to help span the last months before gardens could be harvested again.

The things they brought were exciting, and all the more so after the stand's recent food shortage, but what Mapaline really looked forward to were the merchants themselves. They were not at all like the treeborn in Mapaline's stand. They came from far to the south, from strange lands and strange trees, and brought with them news of the wider world. No matter how many times they had visited and how many nighttime campfires they had gathered round, their stories were always new and always wonderful.

Their visits—once in the spring and once in the fall—were a highlight of the year for Mapaline and her friends, and the caravan was due to arrive any day.

So Mapaline, though she was tired and growing hungry, stayed in the treetop a moment longer to scan the forest for any unusual movement.

Today, on the third day of pruning and watching, she finally saw what she'd been looking for: a shimmer of light off a carriage window on the far hillside. Then another. Then, in an open patch of ground between the trees, she saw the first wagon rumble into view, then a second and a third and a fourth. Each was pulled by several tough looking goats, and walking

A Peculiar Visitor

alongside the whole procession was a scattered group of ten or twelve treeborn.

They were here!

Mapaline scrambled down and began to spread the news. By the time the caravan had made its way across the stream and up their hill, all the treeborn in Mapaline's stand had stopped whatever they had been doing and gathered on the central green.

Mapaline

THE FIRST THING to emerge from the woods, even before the merchants themselves, was their singing. The merchants were always singing, loud and happy and wild, and today the wind carried their song up the hill and through the trees so that their voices arrived long before they did. When they finally pulled into the central lawn, some of the treeborn from Mapaline's stand were singing along—though I'm afraid they didn't know many of the words—and everyone was smiling.

"Welcome!" Ever Fir shouted to the newcomers, and then there were greetings and handshakes and hugs all around. Most of the merchants were well-known to those in Mapaline's stand, but it had been many months and a long winter since they had seen each other last. There were many stories to tell—some good and some sad—and it would be several days at least before anyone got down to the business of barter and trade.

Mapaline scanned the crowd. She was looking for . . . There! Coco and Tumble were two sprouts she always looked forward to seeing. She had never seen a cacao tree—they only grew far to the south—but these particular treeborn were sweet and shy and lots of fun. Mapaline ran over to welcome them.

"How was your winter?" Coco asked. The girls were a bit older than Mapaline, and both of them already had a full growth of stiff, broad, bright green hair.

"It was cold," Mapaline answered. "Very cold. Did you have to travel through much snow?"

"Oh no," said Tumble. "We winter down south and see nothing but rain and sun."

"That's how we like it," Coco said. "I don't know how you manage so far north. Don't you miss the grass and the leaves?"

"Yes, but don't you miss hot tea and warm blankets?"

They all giggled, as girls do, and jabbered on for a few moments about other cold things that the merchants couldn't stand and winter things that Mapaline would never give up. Then Briar and Nettle came up to join them and the reacquainting happened all over again.

"How about a swim in the pool?" Mapaline suggested, and off Coco went to ask permission.

All the merchant roots had made their greetings and were beginning to set up camp. As you might guess, it did not do for a treeborn to sleep on the ground and so, by an ingenious collection of pulleys and ropes and tackle boxes, each of the four wagons could be hoisted up into the lower branches of trees along the edge of the lawn. In fact, Mapaline's stand kept some of the lower branches of these trees cleared for just this purpose. At the moment, four of the goats were pulling the first of the carriages up to where it would be secured safely above ground.

Coco was soon back.

"He says we can go," she beamed. "But I almost forgot. There's someone we want you all to meet. Come on, Ceylon! Come meet our friends."

Over near the waiting wagons, standing off from the roots but not among the sprouts either, was a boy. At the sound of his name he looked and smiled and then trotted over to join them. Mapaline giggled. I'm afraid she couldn't help it and certainly didn't mean any unkindness by it, but the poor boy's legs had clearly outgrown the rest of him and his run was caught somewhere between a trot and a trip. There was certainly nothing *wrong* with him, but like many children—and some trees, I imagine—he'd been growing very quickly and had not yet gotten used to the feel of his new size. Mapaline also laughed because he was as skinny as a twig and because, despite all his awkwardness, his smile made you like him immediately.

And then... well, this part may be hard to explain. For you or me, the last thing we would want someone to remember us by is our smell. I suppose that every once in a while we will spray on some perfume or cologne and hope that others think we smell nice, but mostly we don't want those around us thinking of our "scent" or "odor" at all. If they do, it usually means we forgot to take a bath—or several baths—or that we pulled our clothes from the dirty laundry rather than from our dresser drawers.

It was quite different for the treeborn. Growing things can often make an impression by their smell. Think of a rose or a magnolia blossom, for example. Or even grass that's been freshly cut or the sharp, crisp scent of an evergreen tree. The Wilderness was full of memorable smells, and as the treeborn were very much a part of that Wilderness, they didn't mind if others noticed their own naturally pleasant aromas. In fact, they rather liked it.

So when Ceylon came stumbling to a stop before

A Peculiar Visitor

Mapaline and her friends, despite his gangly legs and warm smile and the kind, confident way he held out his hand to greet them, it was his smell that made the greatest impression. It was a scent that caused them all to stop and look at him twice and then, before introductions could even be made, they all knew what Ceylon's hometree was.

Ceylon was from a cinnamon tree.

Close your eyes for a moment and see if you can imagine the smell of cinnamon. If you want, you can even go out to your kitchen and open your cupboard and take a whiff from the spice rack. There. Do you have it? It brings to mind things like hot cinnamon rolls and warm cider and Christmas, doesn't it? Cookies and apple pie. Maybe, if you're an adventurous eater, it even makes you think of spicy curry or lentil soup.

All this and more are the impressions that followed Ceylon around, and you can imagine the smiles it brought to all the girls' faces. Even the boys, when they had joined the procession down to the pool, could not help but walk closer to their new friend than they normally would have done. It was really very funny. Coco and Tumble and the other merchant children could not help but laugh at them all, and Red even asked a few awkward questions: "Does your skin peel off like a cinnamon stick?" and "Can you smell yourself?" But Ceylon didn't seem to notice that he stood out at all.

"You've not traveled with the merchants before," Mapaline said to him. "When did you join them?"

Coco answered for him. "He's a bit of a mystery. Aren't you, Ceylon?"

The boy smiled again, warm and friendly and not at all offended.

"One morning last fall, just as we were settling into our winter camp, he showed up at our campfire. Looking for a free breakfast, no doubt. He's been traveling with us ever since. And we're glad to have him."

"Yes, but . . ."

Just as you do, Mapaline had more questions but wasn't sure how to ask them without sounding nosy. Or rude. She thought for a moment and then settled on something she thought sounded all right: "Where did you live before that?"

"In the south," he said. "Down by the sea."

"Where are your parents?" Red asked. He was not quite as concerned about prying. Little sprouts rarely are.

Ceylon smiled and looked at the ground.

"He won't say anything about what happened before he showed up at our camp," Tumble said. "It's a big mystery."

"Some stories don't need to be told," he said. For the first time all morning his face changed. He was still smiling, but something else crept in, around his mouth and tightening his eyes. "Some stories only need to be forgotten."

Well. What do you say to that? Nothing, I suppose, and that is exactly what the troop of treeborn sprouts said for some time. Then Red, who was young enough to ask bold questions and also to move on quickly from awkward answers, made a joke about Aker's newly sprouting hair and the teasing was returned and spread to others and soon everyone was feeling

A Peculiar Visitor

comfortable again. Mapaline was very glad to have Red along.

Down the hill they continued, winding along a footpath that ran gradually closer and closer to the river below. Soon they could hear the gentle roar of the waterfall and then the trail led them out into an open space and they could see down the last bit of slope to the waiting pool.

"Oh!" cried several of the visitors at once. "There's a bear in your swimming hole!"

TO BE HONEST, a few of the sprouts from Mapaline's stand had the same reaction. Even those who had ridden Rolf on Short Day had not completely gotten used to his presence, and I think we can understand why. All their lives they had been taught to be very cautious around bears and to avoid them whenever possible. They had been told stories when they were very young about treeborn being eaten up in one gulp by giant grizzlies and told never, ever to get so close to one that they could not outrun it to the nearest tree.

These habits are hard to break—as they should be—and there were not a few of them whose hearts beat a bit faster at the sight of Rolf splashing and rolling in the water below.

Mapaline was just about to reassure them all, but—and this was as much a surprise to her as it will be to you, I suppose—Ceylon reassured them first.

"It's all right," he said. "I think he's friendly." And

then he was off again, continuing down the trail as if it were the most natural thing in the world.

Mapaline and her friends exchanged a look and then followed close behind.

At the edge of the pool, the boy stopped. Rolf, too, stopped his splashing and swimming and floated in the middle of the pool. His fur was wet and matted and dripping. Mapaline could tell that he was trying very hard not to smile.

"Hello, children," Rolf said.

"Hello," said Ceylon and then a few nervous moments later, the rest of the merchants said hello too.

"He's my friend," Mapaline explained. "Really. He's not a normal bear."

"Hrrrmmn," Rolf grumbled—most of the merchant children took a step back at the sound—and then he said, "Not *normal*, Mapaline?"

She laughed. "You know what I mean, Rolf."

"Come in, children," Rolf called. "The sun is warm and the water is *very* cold." Then he rolled over and dove under again, sending water high into the air.

"Come on!" Mapaline cried to the others and charged off the edge to make a splash that would have been much more impressive had Rolf not just made one ten times larger. When she came up again, all the other children were still standing on the edge, staring. Except Ceylon. He was already shivering and sputtering in the water beside her. It was very strange how he seemed to trust Rolf so easily, but before Mapaline could ask him about it, Aker and Red had jumped in to join them. Then Nettle and Nut Birch (Thatch had stayed home as his leg was not fully healed), and after a moment all the sprouts from Mapaline's stand splashed and laughed in the water. There were so many of them that Rolf was obliged to climb out lest he accidentally clobber someone, but he said he was ready to warm up anyway.

Though they were still nervous, Coco and Tumble and the other merchants eventually worked up enough courage to climb carefully into the pool. But they stayed near the edge, as far as they could be from Rolf, who was now sprawled out in the grass on the far side. In time they ventured farther out to splash and play with the others, but if you had really paid attention, you would have seen that each of them kept one eye on the bear at all times. One eye and half a mind, just in case they had to spring away on short notice.

BY THE TIME Rolf had completely dried, the sprouts were tiring and a few of them had climbed out to lie in the grass as well. Of these, only Red had the courage to stretch out next to Rolf.

Finally, Mapaline had a chance to talk to Ceylon.

"Ceylon," she said. "How did you know Rolf was safe?"

The boy brushed the wet hair from his face and squinted his eyes to think for a moment.

"Well," he said. "How did *you* know? The first time *you* saw him."

Mapaline had never thought about this. In fact, as she tried to now, it was very hard to sort it out exactly.

She could only remember that when she had found him nosing about in the underbrush last spring, she had gone right up to him and said, "Hello, bear. What are you looking for?" and that she had not been particularly surprised when he had responded, "Hello, Mapaline. I'm Rolf. I'm looking for lunch."

It took a few moments for this to run around her head several times, and all the while Ceylon treaded water and waited. He looked very silly, what with his gangly limbs thrashing and waving at the water to keep himself up, but all the while it seemed that the pool became more and more fragrant, like tea steeping in a mug of water, and so you hardly noticed how he looked at all.

Finally, Mapaline said, "I guess I don't know. He just looked . . . I just felt . . ." She stopped and scrunched up her face.

"Yes, that's right," Ceylon said, as if she had given a really insightful answer. "That's how it was for me too. You just look at him and . . . you know."

They both looked over at the shore. Rolf was sprawled on his back, feet up in the air, snoring.

"Hey, everyone!" Aker stood alongside the top of the waterfall pointing to the west. "I think we ought to head back home. That looks like a bad one."

Downstream from the swimming pool, the two ridges on either side of the waterway gradually lowered until, some many miles to the west, the land was flat and divided neatly by a river that the merchants called the Broomhandle. The clouds in that direction were dark and low and moving fast, covering the sunny sky as one might cover a lantern to darken a room.

A Peculiar Visitor

The treeborn still in the water reluctantly climbed out. They had no towels to dry off with and all dressed in such thin, light clothing that no one bothered with swimming suits like we do in our world. On a normal day, the sun would do its quick work and they would be dry within the hour. Now, though, the sun was already hidden, and with its light went its warmth as well. Some of the sprouts shivered and some—principally those who had gotten out earlier and were now dry—giggled at them.

"Come on," Aker said. He and Nut were the oldest present and were looking upward with some concern. "I think we'd better get a move on. Before it starts to . . ."

Too late. Faster than you can say "thunder and lightning" the storm was upon them, and I'm afraid to say that it was as fierce a storm as any of them had ever seen. The rain came down as if poured from a bucket, and was so thick and hard that it almost hurt to be struck by it. Soon there were little streams and sudden cascades coming off the hills, filling the Silverleaf and swelling it to the edges of its banks. Poor Red was the only sprout caught on the far side, and there was no way he could get safely across on his own.

Thankfully, Rolf was there with him. Red climbed atop his back and held on tight as the giant bear walked downstream a ways and then waded across the rushing water. Then they were both back up on the bank and everyone headed for the trail.

But it was no good. Running water will always find the easiest path to travel, and it is far easier to run down a much-worn footpath than it is to go smashing through tall grass and underbrush; the trail up the hillside had already become a small stream in its own right. The dirt was turned to mud all along the edges, and the water rushed brown and frothy downward toward the river. When that way proved impossible, all the sprouts had the same two thoughts at once: First, they thought of climbing the trees to find what shelter they could beneath the leaves. Second, they thought of the lightning and realized that clinging to a wet tree in a thunderstorm would be even more dangerous than the muddy trail.

Now, I enjoy a good thunderstorm as much as anyone, and so do the treeborn. They are powerful, awe-inspiring things, even beautiful in their own way. But I enjoy them from the safety of my front porch or, if the wind picks up and blows rain in under the roof, from my living room window. The treeborn, too, much preferred to watch the clouds and rain and wind from inside their snug wooden rooms, up off the wet ground and sheltered from the lightning by four walls and a roof.

Being caught in a storm out in the middle of the woods is not nearly as pleasant.

"It's going to be hard to get all the way up the hill in this," shouted Nut. The wind and rain were loud, and every few seconds came a roar of thunder that was louder still. "It's pretty steep to cut through the woods off the trail."

"How about the picnic cave?" asked Aker.

At this point things were beginning to get serious and all the younger sprouts, especially the nervous merchants who didn't know the area, were looking to the older boys for what to do. Nut nodded and off they went, climbing diagonally up the hill in the direction opposite that of the stand. Aker took the lead with Nut and Rolf coming along behind, picking up the younger ones when they fell and generally trying to be encouraging.

The picnic cave was not far away. On a normal, sunny day, it would have taken only five minutes or so to reach it from the pool, but now everything was wet and it had grown quite dark. Little runnels of water crossed their path, collecting water from the hillside and rushing it downward to the river. Once there came the sound of a lightning strike from the far ridge, and two or three times branches fell in front of them and had to be navigated in the gloom.

Still, it was a much shorter distance than it would have been to go all the way back to the stand. Eventually the hill turned, and just above a bare, treeless patch on its side there was an outcrop of stone and a deep crevice beneath it. The picnic cave was a favorite place for warm weather lunches because the ground was clear before it and you could see all the way down the gorge and to the land beyond. It was also deep enough to get back into the shade on a hot day. The dirt floor was smooth and soft and comfortable.

It was a lovely place, though today they all wished that it was a bit bigger. When the last of them had climbed in, those at the back felt rather smashed and smothered and those at the front were still being lashed by the wind and soaked by the blowing rain. Mapaline was somewhere in the middle, wedged between Briar and Nut and almost sitting in Red's lap. It was very uncomfortable. Then Mapaline remembered Rolf.

"What about Rolf!" she cried, but there was a good deal of grumbling and shifting and arranging going on and I'm not sure who was able to hear her. Those nearest the cave opening were still in some danger and trying to push back in, while those who were already in had nowhere else to go and were feeling claustrophobic.

Then, very suddenly, it got dark and quiet, like someone had thrown a thick blanket over the whole crowded mess.

There were shouts and screams while everyone moved and shoved and tried to figure out what was going on, which unfortunately resulted in no one knowing anything at all. Then it was quiet and there was only the sound of heavy breathing. From somewhere at the back came a muffled voice: "Why is it so dark? What's happened?" Mapaline thought this voice might have belonged to Coco.

From somewhere at the front, another voice—Mapaline thought this one might be Aker's—said, "It's Rolf. He's laid himself over the cave entrance to block the storm."

THE STORM LASTED for some time. Long enough, certainly, for everyone to consider how very cramped and stiff they were. The cave smelled of wet clothes and bodies—and cinnamon, which helped more than

A Peculiar Visitor

you might imagine—and everyone was muddy and very much scratched and bruised by their ramble through the woods. All the awkward positions they had been forced into felt more and more awkward by the moment, and at least once someone mumbled, "I think I'd rather be out in the rain," though I'm sure they didn't really mean it.

Finally, after what seemed like hours, Rolf stood up and sunlight streamed into the cave.

"The storm is over," he said, and his voice sounded tired. "You can all come out now."

And so they did. The first few tumbled out very ungracefully and then the rest began to untangle themselves and follow. All of them, even the merchants, were brave enough to thank Rolf and many of them even patted him or scratched behind his ears. Like all animals, he seemed to enjoy this and was soon nuzzling and nosing them as they clustered about him. Despite the storm, he did not seem to be injured.

But he did look bedraggled. One half of him, the side facing the cave, was more or less dry and fuzzy again. The other side, though . . . Oh dear. Imagine yourself as you first wake up in the morning and your hair is pointing every which way. Now imagine that you spray your head with a garden hose, all the while standing in a great wind. *Now* imagine that it's not just your little head but the whole side of a great big black bear, with more hair than you or I could ever dream of.

That's how the other half of Rolf looked.

"Are you all right, Rolf?" Mapaline asked. Ceylon and Red were standing near enough to listen.

Rolf nodded his head slowly. "Only a bit of a storm," he said. "I've been in worse, though I admit the hail did sting."

"Hail!" Mapaline gasped. Only then did they notice the pea-sized balls of ice littering the ground all around them. "Oh, Rolf, you poor thing. I'm so sorry!"

Rolf bent down and nuzzled her face.

"I'm fine," he said, and then he glanced over her shoulder at Ceylon and added, "There are many who have gone through far worse. Hail is not so bad, is it, Ceylon?"

"No, sir," was all the boy said, and for the first time since Mapaline had met him, he was not smiling. As a matter of fact—and it was hard to tell with all the rain and mud—she thought that a tear might have gently streaked his face.

Before she could say anything, though, Aker spoke from nearby. "All right, everyone," he said. "All the roots will be worried about us. Let's hurry home."

When Mapaline turned again, Ceylon seemed back to his normal self and was throwing a long arm awkwardly across Coco's shoulders and laughing as he used his other to demonstrate what a silly position she'd been crammed into. Then Red was doing the same thing and everyone was laughing and the odd moment between the sweet-smelling stranger and her friend the bear seemed to be over.

No one bothered with the muddy trail on the return hike. Instead, they cut straight through the woods, and though it was still a messy business and not a few more scratches were added to their considerable collection, the sun was back up and soon they

A Peculiar Visitor

were all drying and feeling much better. The storm had done its fierce work against their gorge, though: trees and branches were down; rivulets of water still carved their way through the mud; the river roared double strong down its path. It would be some days before they could swim safely again.

Their parents were relieved to see them when the tired and dirty line finally marched into the stand. The storm had been strong here too, but thanks in part to the pruning, the hometrees were all strong and none had been damaged. One of the hanging wagons had swung into a tree and been battered about some, but other than that everything, and everyone, seemed fine.

"Where is your friend?" Coco asked when the excitement had died down. "The, eh . . . the bear?"

"Oh, he's probably sleeping down in his den," Mapaline said. "Or eating."

"Or both." Red laughed as he came up and joined them. "Sometimes Rolf tries to do both at once."

"Actually, I just saw him perched in a tree down the hill," Nettle said. "You know the one he likes to climb? Ceylon was up there with him."

"Oh!" Coco said, somewhat alarmed, but then she seemed to remember again what Rolf had done at the cave and that if he had wanted to eat any of them, he certainly would have done so by now. "I hope . . . I mean . . . Should we go and see if everything's all right? I know it seems like he's always happy, but Ceylon gets sad sometimes. Maybe . . ."

"I think," said Mapaline, "that Rolf knows something about Ceylon. About where he came from, I mean."

"How would he know that?"

There was a pause and the sprouts from Mapaline's stand all looked knowingly at one another and then laughed.

"We have no idea," Mapaline said finally. "But I think that if Ceylon is sad, there's no one better for him to talk to than Rolf."

"Besides, I'm hungry," Red said, and all the others agreed. It had been a long day and swimming—in the pool and against the rain—had worked up quite an appetite.

Dear Journal,

Guess what! The roots began trading with the merchants today and Papa had me try on some new things. City things! My own clothes aren't even worn out, but Coco's father fitted me with new boots and stockings, a new belt knife, and a long, moss-colored cape. They were the most beautiful things i'd ever seen!

At first i thought Papa was just fooling around, but then—i can still barely believe it!—he said they were for me to keep. To keep! i was speechless, and then i thanked him about a hundred times and he finally said not to thank him but to thank Rolf. it turns out, Rolf has been bringing Papa beaver and fox since Short Day, and Papa's been turning them into pelts for trade. i can't even imagine how they kept the secret from me.

Rolf was nowhere to be found today, but i can't wait to thank him. it's funny that he only picked out things for the fall and winter, though, and not for the rest of summer. i wish i could wear them now. when i put them on, i feel ready for an adventure!

Mapaline

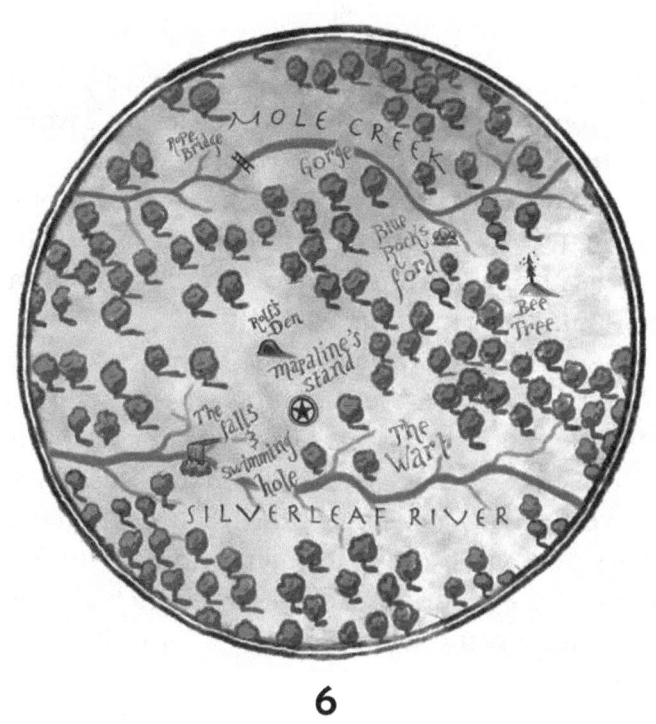

6

An Uncomfortable Conversation

SAYING GOODBYE TO friends, both new and old, was never easy for Mapaline. Though she knew the merchants would return in the fall, she also knew that in the meantime they would all change, just a bit, and have to reacquaint themselves again. That she would miss Coco's stories and Ceylon's wonderful strangeness, and that she was missing, even now, the adventures they were having as they traveled to the next stand while life in her own settled back into its normal routines of chores and schooling and gardening and hunting.

Have I mentioned yet that Mapaline was a hunter? I don't think I have. Well, it may surprise you to know that she was in fact a very good hunter, and it may surprise you even more to find out that this skill was not very remarkable among the treeborn. Practically every treeborn hunted, from little sprouts up, and if some of the older roots or the mothers had moved on to other responsibilities, they could still manage in a pinch.

Mapaline enjoyed hunting with her bow and, as young as she was, had even brought down a flighty sparrow or two last summer along with the more common game like squirrels and mice and beetles. She was also quite good with a fishing spear. Yes, that's right . . . a *fishing spear*! Can you imagine if tomorrow your mother came to you and said, "Dear, we are fresh out of food for dinner tonight. Here. Take this spear, go down to the city pond, and bring back some trout"?

I'm sure you can't and neither can I, but for the treeborn it was a frequent adventure. They had to eat, after all, every day, and there were no grocery stores or farmers' markets at which to shop. It was just them. Alone. In the Great Wilderness. And if they didn't hunt up enough food, well then, they didn't *have* enough food, and that is never pleasant.

An Uncomfortable Conversation

Mapaline was on just such an outing this morning along with her friend Briar Maple. Their mothers had sent them—with their fishing *nets* this time instead of the more dangerous tools—down to the river to catch crayfish.

Unfortunately, this was one of Mapaline's least favorite things to hunt. Crayfish like to hide beneath heavy, difficult-to-lift rocks along the edges of rivers and streams. Also, they have pincers. This means that while one treeborn is holding up a rock and standing knee-deep, or worse, in water and mud, the other is looking very quickly to see if there is a crayfish hiding in the swirling, murky water. If there *is* a crayfish, then they must act doubly quick to snag it before it can grab hold of either of them with its claws. This is not easy because crayfish are as big to Mapaline as a small dog might be to you and prone to fight and thrash and snap like fury. It takes a great deal of effort to finally transfer them to a submerged basket near the shore where they are kept until the hunt is over (crayfish have to be cooked right before eating or they are no good).

In the process of a good crayfish hunt, everyone involved usually gets very wet and very muddy and, most often, very pinched.

Does that sound like fun to you? Well, it didn't to Mapaline either.

The morning had actually gone very pleasantly, but this is mostly because the two girls wasted much time in walking slowly down to the river, talking about how bad the recent storms had been and about how nicely each other's spring hair was growing in and what types of clothing each of them were planning to sew for themselves this summer. By the time they had actually set their big wicker basket in the water among some rocks and gotten to the task of finding a likely stone for lifting, the morning had grown late and the sun hot.

"How many crayfish are we to catch?" Briar asked in a sweet but worried voice. Like Mapaline she was not wearing a hat or hood and the small, leaf-like shoots covering her head trembled in the breeze.

"Five, I think," Mapaline said.

"And they're for dinner tonight?"

Mapaline nodded her head yes and scowled at the water as it rushed by, tinkling noisily and reflecting back the sun. "Aker and Papa are coming down to cook them this afternoon. I think we'd better get busy."

And so they did. The first stone they lifted—Mapaline volunteered for this job to start—was wide and flat and not very heavy. Right away a little pincher reached out for Mapaline's foot, but Briar was quick with her net and soon the first of the crustaceans was lying calmly in the basket. This success greatly encouraged them, so much so that between this first stone and the second stone they took a few minutes to get a drink and a few more to cool off in the icy water and a few more to talk about how very good a nice swim down at the pool would feel.

You know, of course, what was happening. When faced with a job that you would really rather not do, it is often very easy to find many other more enjoyable things to do along the way. This is called procrastinating, and the girls were masters at it.

After they had finally gotten around to checking

An Uncomfortable Conversation

their second stone and then their third, it was almost noon. The sun was now very hot, and when the fourth and the fifth and then the sixth stone revealed no further crayfish, both girls began to think very seriously about lunch. They had not brought anything to eat and knew that to return now would waste quite a bit of time. Too much time. And if there were not five crayfish waiting to be cooked this afternoon, then... Both of them could picture their mothers' stern faces and imagine what punishments might be devised for them. It would be very disagreeable.

"Oh dear!" Mapaline said suddenly as she lowered the seventh rock back into the stream. "I forgot. Rolf was going to give me a ride down to the swimming pond after lunch. And now..."

They looked at each other again and then, miraculously, they found that they could hunt for crayfish with a speed they never imagined.

It was under the twenty-seventh stone, a large and mossy boulder set in knee-high mud, that they found their fourth crayfish. Briar was lifting this time and Mapaline, working quickly and feeling miserable from the heat and the rush and the sinking feeling of missing out on Rolf's visit, was not as accurate as she could have been with the net. First one pincer and then the second grabbed hold of Briar's stomach and then, with the poor girl shouting for the pain of it, the pincers went for Mapaline as well. Somehow Briar managed to keep the rock aloft, and after two or three unsuccessful swipes, and two or three more successful pinches, Mapaline finally caught the creature and wrestled it to the shore.

And then it happened. When one has been procrastinating, there often comes a slim and desperate hope that something—*anything*—will happen to allow you to finally put the chore off for another day. Like when you have been dreading and delaying mowing the lawn and you finally get on your work clothes and push the dirty, smelly mower into the grass and then . . . it starts to rain. You can't mow in the rain. So you put everything away and go in and watch baseball.

I'm not saying this has ever happened to me; I'm just saying it happens like this to some people.

Well, for Mapaline and Briar, it happened. Not rain. You can still hunt in the rain. But just as she and Briar were about to start in on river rock number twenty-eight, there was a call from the far shore.

"Um . . . hello? You there! Hello!"

Both girls looked up to find a huddled band of eight unfamiliar treeborn standing along the riverbank. At first Mapaline felt embarrassed for how she must look: hot and sweaty and covered in mud. But then she saw that the strangers also looked hot and sweaty. Their clothes were dirty and their hair—beautiful, tumbling, flowering hair—was disheveled and pushed flat by traveling hats and packs. These folks had come a long way, and the trip had not been kind.

"Hello?" one of them said again. He was tall, dressed in what must once have been a long, white tunic—it was a long, brown tunic now—and he took a step

An Uncomfortable Conversation

closer to the water's edge. "Are you . . . Is there a stand nearby? Do you live near here, children? We need help."

WHAT WOULD YOU do if all of a sudden you were confronted by eight dirty, bedraggled strangers asking for help on the outskirts of your hometown? You certainly know the proper response. You would immediately shout, "Stranger!" as loud as you can possibly shout and then you would run, as fast as you can possibly run, to your mother or father and tell them all about it. That is the correct response, and you and I have been taught to behave this way since we were old enough to yell and run.

But it was different with Mapaline and Briar. You see, they rarely even *saw* strangers, much less met them alone down by the river. So they did not yell and run. Instead, they did what for you would be the very worst thing to do but for treeborn the most natural: they invited the strangers to come home with them.

Up the hill they trudged, and then Briar ran on ahead to tell the roots what—*who!*—was coming. By the time Mapaline and the newcomers had reached the green, a small crowd was beginning to gather. The Fir brothers were there, and Mapaline's father, and soon there were introductions being made and stories being told and food being hastily prepared. The crowd grew and so did the general excitement. It was all very wonderful, and not only because Mapaline's failure to catch five crayfish was sure to be forgotten. She was also given lunch and found herself eating next to a strange and quiet girl her own age with bright pink and white flowers blossoming from her hair. They didn't say anything to each other—the commotion all around them was too great—but Mapaline tried, by smiles and by sharing the tastiest bits of her lunch, to show friendliness to the poor creature. She had clearly been through a lot.

Then, just as things began to calm down and the travelers' story was being passed along from older roots to younger sprouts, Rolf ambled onto the green.

Well, you can imagine what happened next. For the treeborn in Mapaline's stand, Rolf's presence was now a common thing. They all liked him, even if he did still make them a touch nervous. For the newcomers, though, the sight of a giant black bear showing his teeth through a big smile was terrifying. Two of them fainted straightaway. Another shakily drew a sword, and Mapaline's new friend became so still that Mapaline began to wonder if she would ever be able to move again.

"It's all right," Mapaline said, and she placed her twiggy little fingers gently on the girl's knee. "He's not like other bears. He's safe."

"Safe?" the girl asked, and here at last she moved, though it was only her lips and her eyes, which darted back and forth between Mapaline and Rolf.

"Well," Mapaline said. "Safe for us, at least. He's my friend."

By this time Rolf was upon them, rubbing a warm, furry-faced hello on Mapaline's cheek and, unfortunately, smiling at the new girl.

"*Eeehhhhhh,*" the stranger whimpered.

An Uncomfortable Conversation

"Rolf, stop smiling."

"Oh, yes," he said in his slow and deep and rumbly voice. "Smiling is a hard habit to give up. It's very unnatural. I'm sorry, child. Have no fear. I'll not bite."

"*Eeeeeehhhhhhhh,*" the girl squeaked again, and so Rolf turned to Mapaline.

"What do we have here?"

"They've just arrived," Mapaline said. "Their family has been traveling for weeks from the far south and west, through storms and heat. Sometimes they were forced to sleep on the *ground.*"

The girl continued to stare, and Mapaline went ahead somberly with the story she had heard the travelers share. "Their stand was attacked in the middle of the night. Many of their friends were killed, and they had to leave with almost nothing but the clothes they were sleeping in."

"Attacked?" Rolf asked, and his face turned suddenly serious.

"They've walked and walked, with hardly anything to eat. Then they stumbled upon Briar and me down by the river hunting crayfish. We brought them here and, then, well . . . here they are. You should have seen how much she ate!"

Rolf studied the girl for several minutes and all the while she stared back, wide-eyed and still and clearly terrified. Mapaline watched them. For a moment Rolf looked very stern and intense, as if he were seeing something in the girl's eyes that was not apparent to Mapaline. Then his eyes softened, and he did something Mapaline had never seen him do before. He leaned forward and snuffed a warm, beary breath on the girl's face and then gently licked her cheek. The idea of a bear licking your cheek might not seem very comforting, and in our case it would probably be cause for alarm, but this was different. This was a gentle, calming kiss. A powerful thing. A kiss as only Rolf could give.

The girl immediately relaxed. For the first time she smiled, and it was a wonderful smile, even as dirty as she was.

HER NAME WAS Saela Magnolia, and once she had been fed and bathed and dressed in some of Mapaline's clothes, she was perhaps the most beautiful girl Mapaline had ever seen. All of the strangers, in fact, were quite beautiful, but none so much as Saela. If you have ever seen a magnolia tree in the springtime, you can perhaps understand when I say that the child's smooth, grayish skin and the large pink and white blossoms of her hair had an effect on anyone who saw her. The effect was usually to stop. And then to smile. And then to breathe in deeply the sweet scent of spring.

The two families—for that is what the eight strangers divided into—were split up among the several trees of the stand, and it fell to Mapaline's family to house and care for Saela until it was decided what would become of them all. Having the girl stay in her home, and sleep in her own room, was lovely. Saela was sweet and kind. She had many exciting stories to tell of their escape and their adventure traveling through the Wilderness. Once they had almost been eaten by a pack of wolves as they lay sleeping on the

An Uncomfortable Conversation

ground. Twice they almost drowned crossing rivers, and in one case it was Saela herself who had thrown in a branch to save her father.

But Mapaline could tell that beneath the smiles and the beauty, Saela was very sad. Sometimes she would stop in the middle of a story, especially the stories of the night when they had all left their home, and tears would come to her eyes and she would not be able to continue. At times like this, Mapaline soon learned to give the child a hug and talk about something else. Something happy and bright. After a few minutes, Saela would begin smiling again and be back to her normal self.

Have you ever met someone for the first time and, after speaking with them for only a short while, you feel somehow like you have known them for many years? Or that you would very much *like* to know them for many years to come? They fit you, like honey goes with tea or butter with bread or cream with fresh strawberries. It was like that with Mapaline and Saela. The girl began helping with daily chores and learning to play the games that Mapaline and her brothers enjoyed and acting generally like one of the family. She even got used to Rolf, who stopped by every other day or so to check in on them.

After three weeks of this, however, something began to change. Well, that's not exactly true. Saela was just the same. She was just as friendly and lovely and helpful and sweet. But Mapaline began to feel grumpy around the girl. Subtly at first, a tinge of annoyance here and a flash of crossness there. She certainly didn't *want* to be unkind, but the more she tried not to be irritated, the more she felt her irritation growing. It was very frustrating. She *liked* Saela, after all. What was there not to like?

If you had asked her, Mapaline would not have been able to explain what she was feeling. I think I can, though. Let me try.

It all started with Aker. Mapaline loved Aker very much. He was her big brother, and though he sometimes teased her and sometimes would not let her come out with him and his friends, he cared for her a great deal and they spent quite a lot of time together. He watched out for her on hunts and on rambles through the forest. If he happened to get the last of the honey rolls at breakfast, he would always split it in two so Mapaline could have another half more. And if Mapaline had a bad dream—which she didn't have very often, of course, as she was too old for such things except for when it was extra dark or extra stormy—it was Aker's bed she would climb into to keep safe till morning.

After Saela arrived, though, Aker seemed . . . well . . . *different*. It was just little things, really. Somehow or other the chairs got rearranged at the dinner table so that Saela's seat came between Mapaline and her brother. Somehow or other Aker was more eager to play cards late at night if Saela was also going to play, or to go down to the pool if Saela was going down, or even to volunteer for extra chores if Saela was also doing them.

This was somehow irritating to Mapaline. She didn't really know why. It just was.

Then Mapaline started to notice that others, too,

An Uncomfortable Conversation

acted different around their visitor. Red would still show Mapaline the little bits of treasure that he was always finding, but sometimes he would show Saela first. Briar Maple no longer invited just Mapaline to come with her to hunt or to gather berries; it was always Mapaline *and* Saela. Even Rolf seemed overly interested in the girl and her story and often asked her to walk with him for a few moments when he visited the stand. Just her! Without Mapaline even along!

Perhaps, knowing all this, we can understand Mapaline's grumpiness better. We might feel grumpy too, in her place. Mapaline tried her best to squelch it. She tried her hardest to speak kindly to Saela. To remember all that she had been through. To be patient and continue to share her things and laugh at the girl's sweet jokes and not mind that there were never as many honey rolls to go around anymore and that the extras always seemed to make it onto Saela's plate and not her own.

She tried, but I'm afraid she didn't have much success.

One sunny afternoon Rolf asked her to take a walk with him. She was excited about this, because he had not asked Saela, but she also saw in his eyes that he had something to talk to her about. Something serious. She knew, in short, that she was about to get a "talking-to."

"Why don't you like Saela?" Rolf asked as they left the stand and started down the hill.

Mapaline scowled. "I like her just fine."

"Really?" Rolf said.

"Well, yes. She's wonderful. She's beautiful. Everyone likes her."

"*Hmmgrmm*," Rolf rumbled in his grumbly, beary way.

Mapaline went on. "What's there not to like? She shares. She helps with the chores. She's even good at crayfish hunting. "

"*Hmmmgrrmmmm*," Rolf grumbled again. Then he glanced over at her and said, "But . . ."

Mapaline had said all these sweet things, but the face she made when she said them was not particularly nice. Now she ducked under a fallen branch and walked a few more steps in silence but knew all the while that Rolf was watching her and waiting for her to say more.

"Well," she said finally, "I *do* like her. It's just that everyone else likes her too. Even more than they like me."

She said this last part very quietly and knew at once that even though she had never really thought it out before, it was exactly what she was feeling. She expected Rolf to say something like "That's not true" or "You don't really mean that," but he didn't say anything, so after a few more steps down the hill she went on.

"Everyone is always talking about her hair and how beautiful it is. No one mentions my silly hair anymore. All I have are plain green strands and she has these beautiful flowers. And she is so cute. And her skin is so smooth. And . . . well, I suppose this all sounds silly and jealous."

Now she expected Rolf to say "No, not at all" or

An Uncomfortable Conversation

"What you're feeling is very normal" but instead he said, "That's true. It does sound that way."

"Well, Aker wants to spend all his time with her and I think he's in love with her. And you don't even take walks with me anymore."

"You mean like we're doing now?"

Mapaline didn't have an answer to this, and so she picked up a stone and threw it into the woods as hard as she could. She was feeling something more than jealousy just now. She was beginning to feel angry.

"Everyone likes her more than me and I just wish she would go away! Actually, I wish she never would have come. Maybe I shouldn't have invited them to our stand at all. I should have just said, 'Sorry, no room here. Keep walking and find some other stand to move into.' Then maybe she wouldn't have to sleep in my room and wear my clothes and eat my honey rolls and . . ."

A sound came from Rolf then that Mapaline was *certainly* not expecting. It was something more than a grumble. More than a rumble.

I'm afraid it was a growl, and it stopped Mapaline in her tracks.

HAVE YOU EVER had a dog growl at you? I mean, *really* growl. It's frightening, isn't it? Even if it comes from a silly little dog, a poodle or a Chihuahua, a good snarl can put up the hairs on your neck and cause you to take a step backward.

Now imagine that instead of a dog standing at your knee it was a bear standing high above your head.

Mapaline knew that Rolf would never, ever hurt her, but the sound coming from his throat was still frightening, and for some time she said nothing. She stood still, looking down at her bare toes.

"I know another sweet little treeborn," Rolf said finally, and in a voice much gentler than his growl had been. "She is loving and kind. Strong like a tall maple tree and as gentle as a sapling blowing in the breeze. But she is not acting sweet and loving and kind right now."

Mapaline kicked at a dirt clod. For a long moment she could not think what to say. There were so many feelings and thoughts and words bouncing around inside her head that she simply could not sort them out. You know how this feels, don't you? When you are *feeling* one thing and *thinking* another and very much *wanting* a third. When you know what is right but can't quite figure out how to do it without ignoring other things that seem right as well. When your mind seems to be taking both sides of the same argument all at the same time.

Finally, with Rolf patiently waiting, Mapaline felt that she simply must say something aloud.

"I want to be special," she said. "I want to be special and Saela is so special at everything that nothing is left for me. I don't measure up."

"Measure up?"

"Yes. I don't measure up to her. In anything."

"Hmm." Rolf smiled and then caught himself and nuzzled up to her instead. "May I tell you what I think?"

An Uncomfortable Conversation

Mapaline nodded.

"First, I will tell you that Saela is not the measuring rod. When our lives are examined, they will not be measured against anyone, even that sweet child. It will not matter whether you are *as kind as* Saela. Or *as gracious as* Saela. Or *as loving as* Saela. It will only matter whether or not you are kind and gracious and loving in the truest sense of those words. It will not matter whether you are *as beautiful as* Saela. It will matter what you do with the beauty you have been given and if you use it for good or evil. Do you understand? You and Saela will not be held up against one another or anyone else, but against these things, and I'm sure that there is plenty of room for growth in you both. In all the treeborn everywhere."

Mapaline kicked at the dirt clod again and this time it went tumbling down the hill. This all made sense to her. Rolf always seemed to make sense. But making sense in the head and making sense in the heart are not always the same, and she still didn't *feel* better.

As always, Rolf knew this as well.

"The second part," he said, "the way that others treat Saela and how they treat you, is perhaps a bit more complicated."

Mapaline nodded. "Everyone likes her more than me."

Rolf snuffed out a breath that was partly a sneeze and partly a laugh. "That is certainly not true. Your parents would never love another child as much as they love their own. Red adores you even if he is distracted by a new friend. Just as Briar and Nettle are perhaps distracted for a while. But Saela will not be the *new* friend for long and eventually things will return to normal, only you will have added one more to your group, and having more friends is certainly not worse than having less. As for Aker . . . You will always be his sister and he will always love you, though you know as well as I that he is a boy and eventually his heart will go in a different and special way to a girl like Saela. But not yet. Not quite yet."

"And you?" Mapaline asked. She looked up, so far up, into Rolf's face. "What about you, Rolf?"

Have you ever tried not to smile? It is very difficult, and though Rolf had been working so hard at breaking the habit, when Mapaline asked this last question, he could not help but grin.

But Mapaline was not frightened. Despite the long teeth and the upturned lips, she knew the look for what it was and smiled back.

"The answer to that question is far deeper than you could ever imagine, child. But the short answer is that you are special to me in a way that no one else is, treeborn or otherwise. You are my friend, my best friend if you'd like to call it that, and there is nothing you will ever do that can change that."

"Nothing?"

"Nothing."

"Ever?"

"Ever. To the end of your days."

Do you know that, as silly as it sounds, this assurance from Rolf made more difference to Mapaline than all the very wise and important things he had ever said to her? Isn't that funny? Isn't that amazing? Isn't that wonderful?

Mapaline gave Rolf a big hug then, and with the big, soft pads of his paw he squeezed her right back. Then they continued their walk, and nothing more was said about jealousy or grumpiness or anything serious at all.

When they got back, Saela and Aker and a few of the other children were playing a game of Squirrel and Fox on the green and Saela ran right over to Mapaline and Rolf to invite them in. Rolf is not very good at Squirrel and Fox—he is much too big and slow to be the squirrel and much to terrifying to be the fox—and so he said his goodbyes and went home to his den for a nap.

But Mapaline said yes and took Saela's hand and went and had a wonderful time.

Dear Journal,

Rolf gave me a good talking-to today and it was not very fun. As a matter of fact, it was a bit frightening. But if he had not . . . well, if he had not, then i would still be acting like a little fool. i'm glad he loved me enough to tell me i was wrong.

        Mapaline

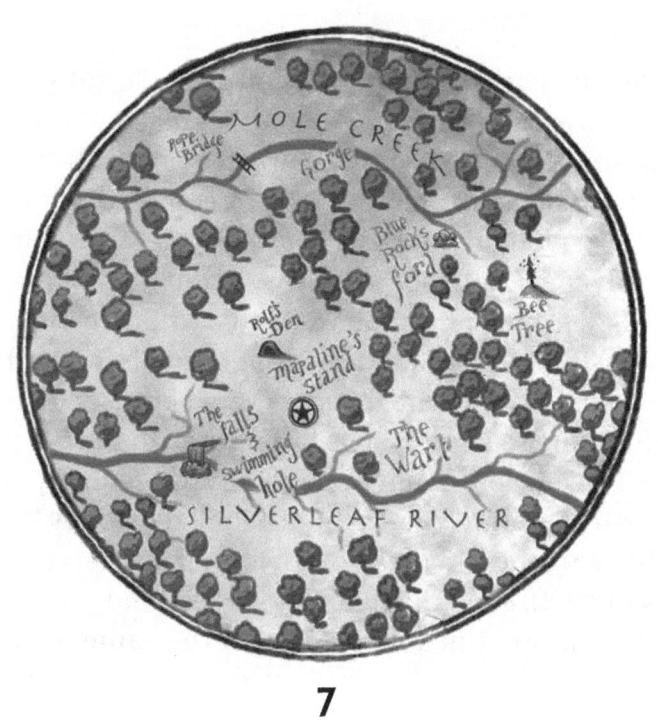

7

Sighting at the Bee Tree

I LIKE HONEY. Do you? On toast or in your tea or mixed with peanut butter and made into a summertime sandwich. It's golden and sweet and sticky and delicious. It's also good for you. And it's also ...

Well, you get the idea. It's pretty wonderful stuff. I suppose that somewhere in this great wide world there is someone who doesn't like honey, but they are missing out, aren't they? If by some unfortunate chance you are one of those strange people, then I really must warn you: this story about Mapaline and Rolf is principally about that golden harvest of the bees. But it is also about an important discovery that they made, one which figures very centrally to their story, and so I hope you will endure all the honey talk.

Now, when I want honey, I simply go to my cupboard and find the glass jar labeled "Honey" and drizzle some wherever I want it. Or if my jar is empty (sad day!), I run down to the grocery and purchase some more. I'm sure it is much the same for you. In either case, there are no trees or hives or bees involved.

As I'm sure you've guessed, it is not nearly so easy for Mapaline and the other treeborn to get honey. To be sure, they love it just as much as you and I. Maybe more. But when they want some honey, they first have to find a large beehive. Then they have to climb the tree, though this part is much easier for them than it would be for us. Then there is the whole matter of the bees, who are never happy about giving up their hive and its contents, and the sticky business of cutting and bagging the honey comb, hauling it back to the stand, pressing it into jars, and cleaning up the very significant mess that all this created.

Then they can enjoy their honey.

It was with very much of this process in front of

Sighting at the Bee Tree

them that Mapaline and Aker and Rolf walked into a sunny clearing on a hot mid-summer day. They had walked all morning, and now stood still, resting and staring up at the tall, sparse pine growing all alone in the center of the grassy space. There was nothing especially interesting about the tree itself. They'd passed hundreds just like it on their hike. But about three-quarters of the way to the top of this particular pine tree, stuck between two long, spindly branches, was a beehive.

"Do you think you can reach it, Rolf?" Aker asked.

For a long moment Rolf stared upward, and then slowly he turned his head to look at the boy. "I am a good tree climber," he grumbled deeply. "But I am also growing fat around the middle. I'm afraid I would break the tree long before I reached the hive."

"You have grown a little chubby," Mapaline said without looking away from the treetop. Rolf grumbled and growled, and though Aker unconsciously backed a step away, Mapaline giggled at her friend.

"It just means there's more of you to love," she said and hugged one of the bear's thick, furry forepaws. Rolf grumbled again and pretended to be grumpy, but they both knew that he was nothing of the kind.

"I guess it's up to you, Aker," Mapaline said.

Now you've heard it said that a person's face turned pale upon thinking some troubling or frightening thought. It was not exactly the same for the treeborn, whose skin was not like ours but thicker and tougher and somehow more barkier and treelike. All the same, there was a definite change that came across Aker's face when Mapaline suggested that he be the one to retrieve the hive. All through their long walk he had been hoping that the tree they'd been told about would be of sufficient thickness for Rolf to clamber up and feeling anxious about the possibility that it would not be. I'm sure you've felt the same over some unpleasantness that you hoped to avoid but were afraid you could not. It isn't a very nice feeling and had made the summer walk far less enjoyable than it might have been.

It was not the height of the tree that bothered Aker, of course. It was the bees.

"Um," he said. "Well, yes. I would. But . . ." Then he paused, staring upward, and said, "Um," again, all the while shifting his feet nervously and backing away by inches from the tree.

"You don't like honey?" Rolf asked.

"He doesn't like bees," Mapaline said.

"Bees?" Rolf looked at the young treeborn and raised his bushy eyebrows.

"They're so big and . . . buzzy," Aker said.

"If only Saela were here to see this," Mapaline began, but her brother scowled at her and the rest of the teasing was choked back. Saela had been busy with other chores today and Mapaline was happy to have her brother all to herself so it was a foolish joke to make. Besides, she had seen Aker fight off sparrowhawks and root out dangerous snakes from their holes, so she knew he was quite brave.

Just not about bees.

There was a long pause in which Rolf's throat rumbled thoughtfully and Aker felt increasingly silly and Mapaline carefully studied the position of the hive.

"Very well," she said after a moment. "I'll do it. But not before lunch."

MAPALINE AND AKER helped remove the great sacks of empty jars that hung across Rolf's shoulders and then they unpacked the food. Lunch was spread out on a blanket that Mapaline had carried in her pack. There were some wild onions and berries for all three, though Rolf politely excused himself to go and hunt up some more. Considering that he could eat in one meal as much as Mapaline's whole family, he tried to be careful not to overeat his welcome. There was also bread and butter for Aker and Mapaline, and though the bread was fresh and the butter creamy, neither of them could help thinking that it would have been even better with honey.

When lunch was finished and washed down with cool water from a nearby stream, they got back to the business of the hive. Aker was carrying a long knife for cutting the long combs away from the tree and a long rope for raising and lowering a bucket full of the pieces. These he gave to Mapaline, all the while making a great fuss about her being safe in the climb and careful with the knife and watchful of the bees and any other possible dangers he could imagine. This was, you understand, both because he loved his sister and because he felt embarrassed that he was not the one going up.

"Good grief, Aker. I'm fine!" Mapaline said finally, pushing him away before buttoning the thick jacket she would wear and pulling a wide hat down tightly on her head. "It's not the first time I've done this, you know. If you'll remember, I did it the last time you were a mouse as well."

Mapaline knew immediately that she had hurt his feelings. To call someone "a mouse" for the treeborn was the same as you calling a friend "chicken" or "scaredy-cat," and it wasn't a very nice thing to say. Aker stepped back and Rolf gave her a subtle look, but as is often the case, she didn't want to admit she was wrong and apologize as she should have. So she said nothing, and this made everyone feel increasingly awkward as her words hung in the air.

Finally, instead of saying that she was sorry, Mapaline said, "Up I go," and was off.

The tree itself was much taller than Mapaline's hometree, and it was also skinnier and sparser and not as pretty. Part of it, in fact, seemed to be dead, as a whole patch of branches near the top were black and without needles. There were also many branches that had been broken off over the long years of the tree's life and these nubs made for easy climbing.

Mapaline was soon high up where the trunk began to narrow and sway in the summer breeze. Higher still and the warm air ruffled her coat and the brim of her hat and the nearby branches. It was a nice sound, and the feel of the tree moving gently beneath her was a nice feeling, and though you and I (certainly I!) would have been frightened, she felt right at home.

Sighting at the Bee Tree

She was so comfortable, in fact, that when she finally reached the branches from which the hive hung, she paused a moment to take in the view. The clearing in which the tree grew was, on one side, level with the forest around it, but on the other side the ground fell away and a long view of the Wilderness stretched out in front of her. Mound after mound of rolling forest led to a great valley that was hemmed in by dark ridges miles and miles away. The air smelled of all those thousands and millions of trees, and for a moment she closed her eyes and breathed it in.

"Are you all right?" came a small voice from the ground, and Mapaline looked down and waved between her feet to Aker and Rolf. She took one last look at the valley and this time caught something she hadn't seen before, a sharp glint of light from a far ridge.

She smiled. "I can see the Tower!" she called down, but Rolf and Aker were so far away that she couldn't tell whether or not they heard her. The distant tower, to which neither Mapaline, nor her parents, nor probably *their* parents had ever been, was the source of many nighttime stories. It flashed again in the sun and then, finally, Mapaline decided that it was time to get down to business.

BEES ARE VERY useful little insects. Did you know that without bees buzzing from springtime flower to springtime flower we could not have as many apples? Or pears or plums or peaches? What they do is called pollination, and I'm sure some day in school you will learn all about it. Also, without bees we would not have honey, and that would be terrible.

But there is one thing about bees that is not so wonderful, and that is the very pointy part, the stinger. Being stung by a bee is exceptionally disagreeable, and if you have never been stung, I encourage you to avoid it. It hurts, if you can believe it, worse than the nasty shots you have to get at the doctor's office (and the bees do not give you candy afterward!).

Now, the treeborn were far more difficult to sting than you or me because their skin is much tougher and harder to poke through. Think for a minute, though, how frightening a tiny bee can seem when it is buzzing around your head. Then imagine that you are not your normal human size, but much smaller, and that the bee seems the size of a ping-pong ball. And all the time that ping-pong–sized insect is buzzing nearby, you know that if he is lucky enough to hit you just right, just hard enough, he will deliver a sting that might lay you up in bed for a whole week or more.

That is how it was for the treeborn.

These thoughts were running around in Mapaline's head as she pulled from her pocket a little tin case and from her pack a bundle of dried grass and green leaves. Inside the tin was a smoldering ember that Mapaline carefully applied to the driest, fuzziest bits of grass. After a few moments of careful blowing, the bundle was smoldering and smoking. Smoke, for a bee, is like a lullaby for a child or a hot cup of tea for a grown-up. It calms them right down and

Sighting at the Bee Tree

somehow makes them not quite so upset if they've had a rough day.

Smoke in hand, Mapaline began walking out toward the beehive. For the first few yards the bees didn't notice her and she moved as quick as a squirrel down the branch. The hive was out near the end. It was wedged between two limbs, attached at the top and bottom, and as she got nearer, she could smell the sweetness that was dripping from the long row of combs.

At first the bees did not much mind that she was there, but when Mapaline threw the end of her rope over the top limb and began to cut the first long strip of comb away from the tree, they began to get agitated. Their buzzing became louder. Their zooming and their zipping got closer. Despite the smoke from her burning branches, a few of the bravest bees began flying so close that one or two of them bumped into her. This, of course, was a much more powerful bump for Mapaline than it would be for us. For Mapaline, a solid thump from a bee could knock her off her footing, and she was forced to reach up high and grab a wispy sprig to steady herself.

Into the bucket went the first chunk of honeycomb. *Now* the bees were angry. Oh so angry! A few were trying hard now to sting Mapaline and a few more to knock her off the tree and a very many more to scare her off with their loud and ferocious buzzing. For a moment Mapaline almost turned around and gave up the whole thing. I think I might have! But then she remembered that she had called Aker a mouse for being afraid of bees, and she knew that, should she

Sighting at the Bee Tree

run away, he would be tempted to call her the very same thing. The thought of this and of how silly she would look scampering down the tree with nothing to show for her efforts and of Aker standing there grinning an "I-guess-you're-not-so-brave-now-are-you" grin was enough to stop her retreat.

So she took a deep breath and stuck it out. A few more breaths blown into the bundle of grass helped to increase the smoke and a few more slashes to the hive began filling up her bucket. Soon it was brimming with heavy honeycomb and she began to lower it down, down, down to the ground, out of reach of the bees, and then up, up, up it came, ready for another load.

Eating honey, as I think I've mentioned, is very fun. Harvesting it is very not fun. By the time the bucket had been lowered and raised three more times, Mapaline was hot and sweaty and tired and sticky and grumpy. For the most part the bees had calmed down and were now flying lazy, drowsy loops around the tree, but they were still bothersome and a bit dangerous. Even a lazy, drowsy bee might knock Mapaline off the branch. Mapaline was also very thirsty, and the smoke had blown into her eyes several times, which is not at all comfortable.

In short, she was ready to be done.

Once more down and once more up and then Mapaline filled the bucket for the last time. She had harvested a lot of honey, but there was still three times as much—four times!—left for the bees, and so even after the smoke wore off they wouldn't feel too bad.

They'd start rebuilding right away, and in no time at all they'd have forgotten about the whole thing.

BY THE TIME Mapaline reached the ground, Aker had already filled half the jars with the honeycomb. He was almost as sticky as Mapaline: honey covered his hands and was splattered up his arms and smeared here and there wherever he had reached to scratch an itch or brush his hair back from his face. Stuck to all this was dirt and pine needles and even a few unfortunate bugs. He made for quite a sight.

Mapaline almost laughed. Then she remembered that she had already said something rather unkind this morning and decided to bite her tongue. Besides, she didn't look any better.

"You did a good job, Mapaline," Rolf said. "The bees looked angry."

"They were!" Mapaline was taking off her heavy jacket and hat. "I think I have bee fuzz stuck to my face from the ones that kept running into me. Did we get a lot?"

"Yes," Aker said and he smiled at her but she could tell he was still feeling bad about not having done the difficult job himself. He was much quieter than usual.

Mapaline went for a long drink at the stream and then joined him to pack the rest of the honey. They worked quietly. By the time they were done, there were probably sixty clay jars and ten or twenty glass jars full to the brim and capped tightly. They arranged them gently into the sacks that Rolf had carried and

Sighting at the Bee Tree

stuffed in handfuls of (sticky!) grass and leaves to provide some cushioning. Then it was down to the stream for some much-needed washing.

This took quite a while. By the time they were done, the sun was halfway back down the sky and they would have just enough time to get back to the stand before dark.

"You did a good job, Mape," Aker said quietly once they were well on their way. Rolf trudged along behind them, a giant, bulging sack over each shoulder. "You were very brave."

"Thanks," Mapaline said. They walked a while longer and then, finally, Mapaline said what she should have said a long time ago. "You're not really a mouse, Aker. I'm sorry I said that."

"It's okay."

"Really, you're not. You're brave too. Just not about bees."

She smiled at him and he smiled back, and the rest of the walk home was much more pleasant.

THAT NIGHT MAPALINE and her family and Rolf all ate dinner out on the grass in the middle of the stand. A few of their friends were there too, like Saela and Briar and the Birch brothers. Mama Maple had baked bread and sliced up an enormous bowl of summer strawberries and nuts. Everyone put honey on everything and it was all delicious.

After dark, Rolf stood up and said goodbye. Then he asked, "Mapaline, will you walk with me?"

They went away from the stand, down into the woods, and behind them Mapaline's family began a small bonfire that lit the darkened trees of the hilltop.

"Thank you for carrying all the honey," Mapaline said.

Rolf nodded and they kept walking. Have you ever been with a good friend, someone you know very well, and they are so unusually quiet that you begin to get the feeling they have something on their mind? Something they want to say, something important, but they haven't decided just how to say it yet? With every step down the hill, it was more and more like this for Mapaline. Rolf never said a lot, but tonight . . . something was on his mind.

After a few more minutes, Rolf finally spoke. "Mapaline, when you were up in the tree today, you shouted down something about the Tower."

"Yes, I saw a glint of light reflected from it. The sky was so clear and the sun so bright . . . I've only seen the Tower a few times in my whole life."

There was another pause and Mapaline wondered what could possibly be bothering her friend.

"You are sure it was the sun? That the Tower . . . *itself* . . . was not lit?"

"How would the Tower be lit? Do you mean on fire?"

"No, no . . . just lit. Like a lamp shining from the top."

Mapaline thought for a moment, scrunching up her face to try to remember. "I don't think so. I think it was just the sun."

Rolf grumbled a ruminating, thoughtful grumble that did not sound at all satisfied.

"Why, Rolf? What's the matter?"

Rolf gave her a hesitant, sideways glance. "I've been

to that tower many times over the long years. Many times. A friend would sometimes meet me there. When we last parted, he, knowing what I was about, told me that when he needed me, he would signal from the Tower. By lighting its top." He paused for a few steps and then said, "But you think it was just the sun?"

"I think so, Rolf. I didn't see it for long. Why haven't you ever told me about the Tower before? I didn't know you'd ever been there."

Rolf snuffed out a little laugh and said, "There is much I have not told you, Mapaline. And much I plan to tell. The time for secrets, I think, is soon to turn, like the summer into fall."

She waited for more, but when he spoke again, he seemed ready to let the matter drop.

"Very well. Thank you, Mapaline. You were very brave today and the honey was very good. Now, I think, it is time for sleep."

"Good night, Rolf," she said. She hugged his forepaw and felt the pads of his other paw pat her on the head. Then she headed home.

That night, before bed, Mapaline stood at her open window looking out at the stand and the surrounding trees. It was Second Moon and both were already up and shining brightly. Then . . . well, it was strange. She thought she saw, out past the edge of the stand, up high in a tall, strong pine, the black silhouette of Rolf the bear. Looking east.

Mapaline remembered his questions about the Tower.

Rolf, she wondered. *What are you up to?*

That Rolf. He was a very odd bear.

Dear Journal,

At dinner tonight i asked Papa what he knew about the Tower. He said that no one he knows has ever actually been there but that he was always told that it was an old fortress. His grandfather, who apparently had many stories to tell about the Tower, said that there was a great stone road running below it and that the Tower served as a watch post for a kingdom of giants.

But Rolf has been there! How exciting! i'm going to have to see if i can get him to talk about it some more. And about his friend. i wonder . . . is the friend a bear? Or a treeborn like us? Or something else entirely?

Mapaline

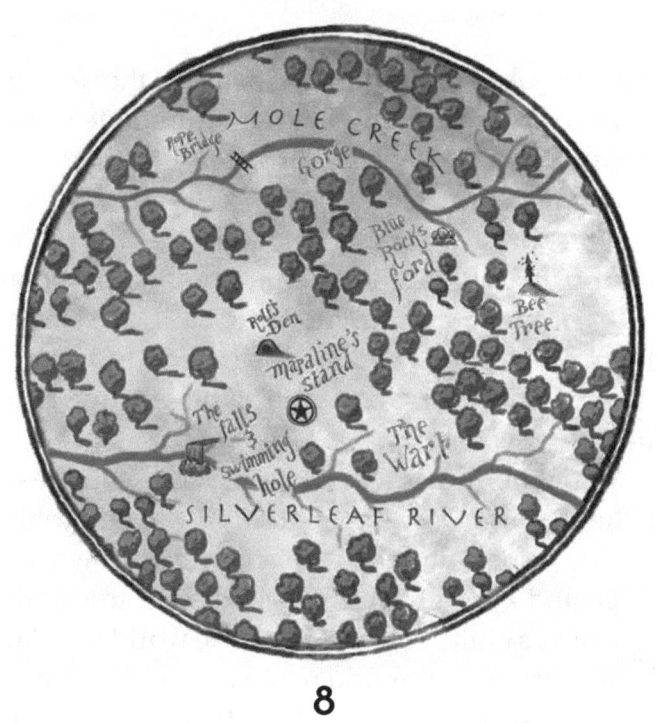

8

Thief in the Dark

WHEN SUMMER AFTERNOONS grew hot and muggy and sticky, the treeborn tended to stay close to their trees. Everyone gave up chores and work for a time to sit in the shade of a big sycamore or lounge high up in the branches of an oak where the breeze was strong and they could close their eyes and be still. They often joked—or at least half joked—that the trees behaved the same way, for as the sun got high, they kept the shade close to themselves and waved their tall branches to catch the wind.

But chores still had to be done. The little patches of crops had to be tended and food gathered and water brought up from the river. So in the summer the treeborn woke early and worked hard through the morning hours to get these things done before the day grew too hot.

Mapaline always felt that doing chores in the cool of the morning was almost—*almost*—as enjoyable as playing. Especially when there was a fog down in the gorge and a mist hovering over distant trees; when there was a chill in the air; when the world was damp from overnight rains and ready to grow twice as fast when the sun finally rose. If you have ever woken on a summer morning in the deep woods, I am sure you felt the same way.

It was still work, though, when you got down to it, and so Mapaline's favorite time of day was not the cool of the morning. Nor was it the restful heat of midday. It was evening. The light lingered in their part of the Great Wilderness, and the long dusk was when the treeborn children went out to play.

What is your favorite game? Hide-and-Seek? Freeze Tag? Capture the Flag? The treeborn children had their own versions of these games, though I suppose they came up with their own names and rules for them all, just like children everywhere. Mapaline's favorite game, however, was Arrows.

I'm sure you have never had the pleasure of

playing Arrows. At least, I don't think so. To play properly, first you need a large and rolling forest. These can be difficult to find, especially in our day when it feels more likely that we will stumble across a parking garage than a patch of old and respectable trees. Second, you must have access to archery equipment—bows and very sharp arrows—and, more importantly, have your parents' permission to use them in play.

I don't know about your parents, but mine never let me play with sharp objects like arrows. So you can see why this game is not at all popular in our world.

Mapaline and her friends, however, were very comfortable with such things and knew how to use them safely and responsibly. And so, when it had been decided that a game of Arrows was to be played on a certain evening, those playing would all gather at the top of a hill, as far from their stand as could be managed depending on how late in the evening it was. Then they would all climb the branches of the tallest tree on that hill and one of them, usually one of the older sprouts, would tie a red ribbon to the end of an arrow and shoot it as high and far into the forest as they could possibly shoot it.

And then the race was on. The first to find the arrow was the winner. You can imagine how this race could go. Sometimes over streams and sometimes over fields. Sometimes into rocky crags and sometimes through thick, thorny bushes. Sometimes the arrow would be found stuck fast to the branches of a tall pine and sometimes half buried in a muddy rain puddle. Sometimes it would not be found at all, and though this was a touch disappointing, it did end the game in a tie for everyone and there was some satisfaction in that.

Tonight, after several straight days of storms followed by a day of the hottest, muggiest weather you can imagine, the children were more than ready for a good game of Arrows. It was a perfect night for the adventure. First Moon was up and full so that, even after the sun had finally set, there would be some light left for the end of the hunt and for finding their way home afterward. It was breezy and cool and clear. The children had gathered east of the stand on a little nub of a hill they called "The Wart." At the top of the Wart, like a terrible, crooked hair, grew an old and gnarled oak tree. A lonely tree, but not so lonely once eight treeborn had clambered to its top.

Mapaline and her older brother were there, as were Aker's friends Nut and Thatch Birch. Nettle Fir had come, though not her brother, Rollwater, because he was sick. Briar had come as well, and so had Saela and another of the newcomers, Everbright, who was a year or two younger than Mapaline. Saela and Everbright used to play a game just like Arrows at their old stand, though they had called it Freefall and used yellow ribbon rather than red. Also, they had always hunted in pairs in their version of the game, which Mapaline and her friends found odd. Still, they had paired up for tonight's game because the new girls did not know the land as well as the rest and would have had small chance of winning on their own. Everbright was going to be with Briar, and Saela with Mapaline. Aker—who had wanted to partner with Saela but had not been quick enough in the asking—was going to shoot the arrow.

"All ready?" Aker asked. Everyone said that they were and turned away from the sun to face east. The treetop swayed gently, and for a moment—just a moment—all the chatter stopped and there was quiet as Aker fitted his arrow to the string. Saela squeezed Mapaline's hand and they smiled at one another and Mapaline was very glad that her jealousy had worn off. It was much more fun this way.

"Here we go!" Aker pulled back on the bowstring as far as he could pull and then, with a loud *twang*, off went the arrow with its red ribbon fluttering behind. Then it was quiet again as all eight children watched carefully to try to see where it would fall. The shaft was so small and the distance so great that none of them could be absolutely sure, but Mapaline thought it had gone just across the stream that wound around the bottom of the hill, down near the rapids where the blackberries grew.

Once the prize had disappeared, everyone turned back to Aker, who slowly placed his bow over his shoulder and secured it to his light shirt with a tie or two. Then, after a deep breath, he shouted, "Go!" and they were off.

Down the tree, off the Wart, and tumbling pell-mell toward the shallow valley into which the arrow had flown. Soon the pairs had begun to separate from one another, each choosing a different path to reach the place where they thought they had seen the arrow fall. All the while there was the sound of laughter, sometimes near and sometimes far, and the occasional crash and tumble through an unexpected bush or patch of tall grass. By the time Mapaline and Saela reached the stream, the closest competitors were upstream from them some ways and could just be heard splashing through the water to get to the other side.

"We can swim across here," Mapaline said.

"Swim? But we'll be soaked."

Mapaline laughed. "Yes! It's not nearly as fun when we don't get to swim."

This seemed very strange to Saela, who had never had to cross streams when playing the game where she had grown up, but it seemed fun too, and she was laughing as she took a string from her pocket and tied up her thick hair. It was no longer flowering, of course, as the blossoms fade with the springtime. In their place was hair like thick, green leaves and she almost looked silly with them tied up in a bundle at the back of her head. As silly as a girl like Saela can look, anyway. Mapaline giggled and shook her own hair out, untangling the broad strands so they would dry more quickly after their plunge. The water was cold and moved gently here, just over their heads, and they were soon across, chilled in the breeze and with their light, linen clothes drying far faster than their hair.

"This way!" Mapaline called and they took off upriver along the shoreline.

Now you might think that finding an arrow that is no longer than your forearm and has been shot at random into the woods is an impossible task. Especially with the daylight fading and moonlight slowly taking over. But you must remember that for the treeborn, the arrow was not "very small" but "very normal" and their eyesight is better than ours and more used to scanning the woods for little things that seem out of place. They do this all the time when hunting and can sometimes spot a green beetle on a green leaf at a distance that would astound you. I know that it has astounded me.

It was not so very surprising, then, for Mapaline and Saela to find Aker and Thatch standing below a big oak tree and staring up at the place where the arrow had stuck fast. A boulder was lodged in the dirt on which the tree grew, and long roots crawled down and around the stone, finding their way into the earth whichever way they could. What *was* surprising was that the boys had not yet pulled the shaft out and claimed victory.

"I think you cheated," Mapaline said, but she was laughing and didn't really mean it. It was what they always said whenever the winner was the person who had shot the arrow. Aker smiled, and grinned wider still when he saw Saela.

"Ha!" he said. "We won even *with* Thatch's bum leg!"

Thatch protested this and aimed a kick at Aker to emphasize that his leg wasn't "bum" anymore, but it was all in good fun and everyone laughed.

"Anyway," Aker said, "look at this." He held out his hand and in its palm was a golden chain. Attached to it were three silver maple leaf pendants.

Mapaline held the chain up so that the leaves

dangled from it. "This looks just like the one Mama lost this spring."

"It *is* the one mother lost. Papa had it made especially for her. I'm sure there's none like it anywhere, and certainly not near our own stand."

"But where did you get it?"

Aker pointed toward the base of the oak tree. Just below the arrow was an open space in the earth between one of the roots and the boulder. "It was just lying there. In the opening of that little cave."

The four of them stood quietly for a moment, thinking and staring at the hole.

"But how would her necklace get all the way out here?" Saela asked. "I've never seen your mother go this far from the stand in all the weeks I've been here."

"No, she never does," said Aker, and then, "I bet I know. I bet we have a thief on our hands."

"A thief?" Saela said, and she took a step closer to Mapaline. "Do you really think so?"

"Yes, it's happened before. I bet Thatch and Mape remember. Three or four years ago odd bits and bobbles started disappearing from the stand. Strange things, like a spool of orange thread and a spoon. Remember? Briar's mother lost a hairpin that she'd been given by her grandfather. How she carried on! And no one could figure out where all these things were going."

"Yes, I remember," said Mapaline. "It was a raccoon!"

"That's right. Later that year we saw him carrying off a hat that had been left on the Birches' roof. We followed him home and found a whole treasure trove—things that had been missing for a year or more. Some things we had never seen before, stolen from who knows where. And I'll just bet . . ."

He stepped toward the hole and bent over to peer inside.

"Don't you dare, Aker Maple," Saela said.

I think I should stop here and explain something. In our world we have things called "unwritten rules." Unwritten rules are things that everyone knows to do or not to do, even though there is not necessarily a law somewhere explaining it. An unwritten rule would be: When you see a little old lady about to cross a busy street, you take her arm and help her make it safely across. Or: Don't go swimming right after you've eaten. Or: When company comes over for a visit, offer them something to eat and drink. These are unwritten rules.

Well, among the treeborn it is an unwritten rule that you should never crawl into an animal's den unless you know very well *what* kind of animal it is and whether or not it is at home. You can certainly see the sense in this. Any number of creatures could live in a hole the size of the one the four friends had found, from raccoons and squirrels to snakes and foxes, and most of these creatures would not appreciate a surprise visit from a nosy treeborn.

Aker knew all this, and was just about to give up the idea of going inside when Thatch's brother, Nut, arrived with Nettle Fir.

Aker began to fill them in, but before he could finish, Nettle said, "I'll bet that's where my teacup's gone!"

When the merchants had visited in the spring, Nettle had traded in a pinch of gold dust for a beautifully painted porcelain tea cup. It was white with blue and green vines growing all around the outside and down the handle. A few weeks ago, the cup had disappeared, and though everyone thought that Nettle had probably taken it out for a picnic and lost it, she claimed it had been sitting on top her dresser one morning and had disappeared by evening. It now seemed, perhaps, that she wasn't as forgetful as they had thought.

"Please, please, Nut. You must go in and get my teacup! I'm sure that's where it's gone."

Nut stood still a moment, scratching his head's foliage and looking very seriously at the dark hole in the ground. The light was fading fast now, and though the moonlight was bright, the dusk made the cave seem even deeper and darker than it had a few moments ago. He knew of the unwritten rule as well as Aker did, but . . .

Well, I'm afraid there is something strange about boys. Especially boys of Nut and Thatch and Aker's age who are in the company of girls of Mapaline and Briar and Saela's age. Though they may be boys of good common sense, as these three certainly were, something can come over them in a flash that makes all their clear, wise thinking turn silly and foolish.

This was, perhaps, the first time any of these six treeborn children had experienced this phenomenon, and none of them were at all prepared for it. Before they knew it, an impulse to be brave and courageous had swept over the boys. The girls saw it happening, all before their very eyes, but didn't yet know how to talk their friends out of their urge to show off. And so, very unexpectedly, the simple game of Arrows had turned into something else entirely.

"I'll do it," said Aker suddenly, and Nut and Thatch immediately began gathering long sticks and dry brush to make him a torch.

"Aker, you can't go in there!" cried Mapaline. "What if the raccoon is home?"

"Or what if it's not a raccoon at all?" said Saela. "It could be anything!"

"Oh, it's probably nothing at all," said Nut as he wrapped a length of string around and around the leaves and bark of the torch. "Probably nobody home and all he'll find are little chambers . . . filled with treasure!"

He said this last bit with a glint in his eye, and the glint passed quickly to Thatch and Aker. In a moment they had struck some flint to start a smudge fire and were all gathered around the black entrance speculating about how deep the cave was and how many rooms it might contain.

This was really too much for Mapaline. It was like . . . like . . . well, it was like falling. You know: that very brief moment, right after the slip and before you have truly crashed to the ground, when your mind sees what's coming. When you know, in a flash, that you've lost your balance and are about to take a tumble and there's nothing you can do about it. Somehow, even though this moment doesn't last longer than it takes to blink your eyes, you also know how foolish you are going to look and how much it is going to hurt and that you should have walked around the patch of ice but you didn't and then . . . *Slam!*

For Mapaline this whole situation was a bit like that. She knew there was trouble coming. Knew it as clearly as the tripping person knows the ground is rushing up to meet them, but there was nothing she could do to stop it. Everything was happening far too fast.

Then, just at the last moment, right before the torch was lit, Saela stepped toward the cave and put her hand on Aker's arm. "Please don't," she said. "Please. We can all come back tomorrow and have a look, but it's late and getting dark and . . . Oh, please. Let's come back tomorrow." She was really very worried.

Saela didn't know it, of course, but this was bound to have just the opposite effect she intended. In truth, she would have had a far better chance at stopping Aker if she had pretended indifference and began to stroll casually away, off toward the stand without even a note of worry in her steps. This is silly, isn't it? It seems backward. I'm afraid, however, that this is exactly how such things work.

Aker smiled—a big, bold, carefree smile like all boys his age dream of smiling—and then held out his hand for the torch. Nut lit the brand and passed it up and then, with the cheers of the two boys and the pleadings of the three girls ringing in his ears, Aker disappeared into the hole.

For a while we will have to leave Mapaline and the others outside. They stood peering into the cave until Aker turned a corner, and then they sat and waited until Briar and Everbright arrived. And then they sat and waited some more.

We will follow Aker instead. Up until the first turn in the tunnel, he was feeling quite confident. He was stooped down at first, then crawling on his hands and knees with the torch outstretched before him, which was not a particularly comfortable position to be in, but the feelings of bravery running through him made up for all that. After the first turn in the passage, though, he began to feel a bit different. The torch had burned very low already, and now only the glowing tip of the stick let off any light at all. Also, the tunnel was getting more cramped and beginning to smell bad. Then—and by this point he was well into the hillside and no longer under the oak tree at all—the path branched into two directions. He chose the left one, for no particular reason, and was soon crawling almost on his belly in the dirt. The ceiling of the passage scraped along his head, dropping bits of earth onto his face. It was terribly uncomfortable.

By this time, all those feelings that had driven him to explore the cave had significantly faded. Bravery had turned to annoyance, and there was no one here to show off for. Now it was simply dark and smelly and cramped and dirty.

It was time to get out.

But then, just as he had begun to scoot backward, he saw another opening off on his left, and when he stuck what remained of his torch inside, the light from its glowing end set something to glistening. Actually, lots of somethings. He scooted farther into the room and found that his hand rubbed up against . . . a tea cup! Briar's tea cup? Farther on there was . . . he couldn't quite make it out. Bits of gold dust on the ground? And over there something large and smooth. And at the far back he saw two little spots in the dark. Spots like stars, which was silly since he was underground, or pools of water or—

Eyes!

Yes, eyes, and when he heard a *hissss* coming from that direction as well, he was no longer on a fun little adventure. He was in a serious situation indeed. He was in the den of a snake!

Now, throughout this episode, I hope I have not given the impression that Aker was *really* a silly, foolish boy who only pretended to have courage. This is not true. In fact, Aker was a very brave and mature young treeborn who was only *acting* silly and foolish. Beneath all the showing off was still the real Aker; the Aker who had protected his siblings from foxes and helped the old roots hunt down dangerous coyotes and wolves. The Aker who many of the other children looked up to and who many of the stand's parents admired.

It was this Aker who emerged very quickly in the dark of the tunnel. Out came his knife, and though the blade was no longer than your index finger, in Aker's hand it was something any snake should fear. Slowly then—very slowly—he began to back out of the dark room. He was hoping the snake would simply allow him to quietly make his way out of the tunnel. Then they could both go on with the rest of their night happy to be out of each other's company.

But it was not to be.

Like a dragon guarding its stolen horde, the snake seemed angered by Aker's intrusion. The hissing grew louder and the eyes, still just points of light in the darkness, began to move this way and that. Aker scooted towards the exit as quickly as he could, but the serpent was much faster. The eyes grew nearer and nearer and then its scales were visible just up against the ember that still clung to Aker's firebrand. Green and silver, they glistened in the glow. Aker swatted at them with the stick as hard as he could manage, but this put what dim light remained out completely and Aker now found himself wriggling backward in complete darkness.

The snake was still coming. Aker could hear it. As he scraped his way toward the entrance, he kept the dead torch moving back and forth in the passage, back and forth, and whenever it struck something he would lunge forward with his knife and slash at the spot. Most often he struck nothing but the dirt wall, but every once in a while, his blade went home and caused his enemy just enough pain to be kept at bay.

Wriggle and creep and crawl, back and back and back, and soon Aker was in the main passage and headed for the bend in the tunnel. There was more room here and he was able to move faster, all the while probing with the torch and slashing with the knife, and then he came around the bend and the deep darkness lessened. Firelight streamed in from a bonfire his friends had built, and he could hear the wood crackling and popping.

You might imagine that the light would be a great encouragement to Aker. Fighting a snake in the dark is indeed a terrifying experience. But the darkness had also hidden from him the sight of his frightful enemy. No more. In the flickering light and shadow, he now saw the serpent's pointed head and flicking tongue and long, thick body trailing off behind. This proved to be far more frightening than the darkness, and for a moment Aker froze. No more crawling, no more slashing, no more probing with the torch.

It is what I might do at the sight of a snake slithering a foot from my nose. In fact, I imagine that many a mouse and mole had felt just the same way at the sight of this very snake, frozen in place just an instant before they were eaten. The snake knew this and saw its advantage. With a flash of its scales it struck at Aker, like silver lightning in the shadows.

You remember how we talked about falling, and how many thoughts you can think in the blink of an eye? It was like that now. In that instant, Aker remembered Mapaline's and Saela's warnings. He remembered his parents and, for some reason, the taste of warm, sweet maple rolls. He also remembered that he had been struck at by snakes before and *that* memory, faster even than the serpent, jerked his body to the side and thrust both arms outward as hard as possible. The snake missed in its strike and found its head knocked against the tunnel wall by Aker's torch and knife and just as quickly as it had come forward, it retreated back again.

But it was not finished. The loud hissing resumed and the pair was back at it again, squirming and slithering toward the entrance, thrust and strike and parry, and Aker realized for the first time that he was shouting as loudly as he could. He also realized that he was growing very tired and that the muscles in his right leg were beginning to cramp up. He was slowing down, inch by inch, and the snake seemed to sense that the end of its hunt was near. In and out went its tongue, back and forth its head. Closer and closer.

"What's the matter?" someone was shouting from outside, and then Aker heard himself calling, "Snake! Snake! Snake!" over and over.

Then his legs were out of the hole and he tumbled down upon the roots and to the ground. The snake was right behind him, its head out and into the light, rising up and then . . .

A *thump* shook the ground.

When Aker looked up, in place of the snake's head and jaws was a black and furry paw, claws spread wide, pressed heavily into the soft earth.

Rolf. The great bear was up above, holding tight to the oak tree and leaning down just enough to squash the snake beneath his powerful front foot. For a moment a terrible growl hung in the air and Rolf's face, too, had turned from the friendly bear they all knew to something awful and great and frightening. But only for an instant—a frozen instant in which Aker and all the rest of them saw what Rolf *could* be when the need arose.

Then it was over and everyone was gathered around Aker. Mapaline was carrying on about how stupid he had been and Saela was crying and Nut and Thatch were begging for all the details of what had happened.

A FEW MOMENTS later they were all headed back to the stand. Mapaline and Rolf were out in front, across the river and around the Wart with the other children trailing along behind. Now that the danger was over, the whole adventure was beginning to feel exciting and courageous again, and Aker was answering a barrage of questions: "How long was the tunnel?" "Were there more snakes?" "What treasures did you see?" "Will you go back in tomorrow?" Even Saela seemed to have gotten over the fact that Aker had ignored her pleading. She now walked next to him, as eager for information as the rest.

Mapaline, however, was still feeling that her brother had acted very foolishly and was a little annoyed that he was getting so much attention for it. So for the moment, she walked in silence, one hand up high and buried in Rolf's thick fur.

When they'd rounded the Wart and wound their way back to the foot of their own hill, Rolf said, "Mapaline, are you angry with your brother?"

Mapaline thought a moment. She wasn't really sure and said as much.

"I understand," said Rolf and then, after a pause he added, "What he did was foolish. But he is safe now and will learn from his mistake. Everyone acts foolishly sometimes."

They walked a moment more and then Mapaline said, "Do you?"

"Do I what?"

"Act foolishly. You said that everyone acts foolishly sometimes, but you always seem to make the right decisions. Every time."

"*Hmmrmm*," Rolf mumbled and rumbled and thought. "*Hmmmnnrrrnnrmm . . .*"

That was all and Mapaline thought that he wasn't going to answer. But then he said, "Perhaps it would be foolish for me to answer that question."

Mapaline laughed and punched him good-naturedly in the leg. Then she leaned in and snuggled against his fur. "You know what, Rolf? I'm glad I found you."

Rolf smiled—in the dark it was not so frightening—and made an unusually quick decision.

"Mapaline, would you like to know a secret?"

She was still hugging his leg but leaned back eagerly. "Of course!"

"Then here it is: *You* did not find *me*. *I* found *you*. Was *sent* to find you, as a matter of fact, and you were just where I thought you would be."

For a moment Mapaline gaped and then one of a dozen questions spilled out of her mouth, followed by all the rest with hardly a breath of separation between. Rolf rumbled and snuffed out a chuckle.

"Perhaps *that* was a foolish thing," Rolf reflected. "To tell you. But I don't think so. Secrets, though, Mapaline, are like maple rolls: too many at one time will upset your stomach."

And that was all he would say.

Dear Journal,

Rolf is infuriating! Sometimes he makes me want to scream!

But i still love him.

Mapaline

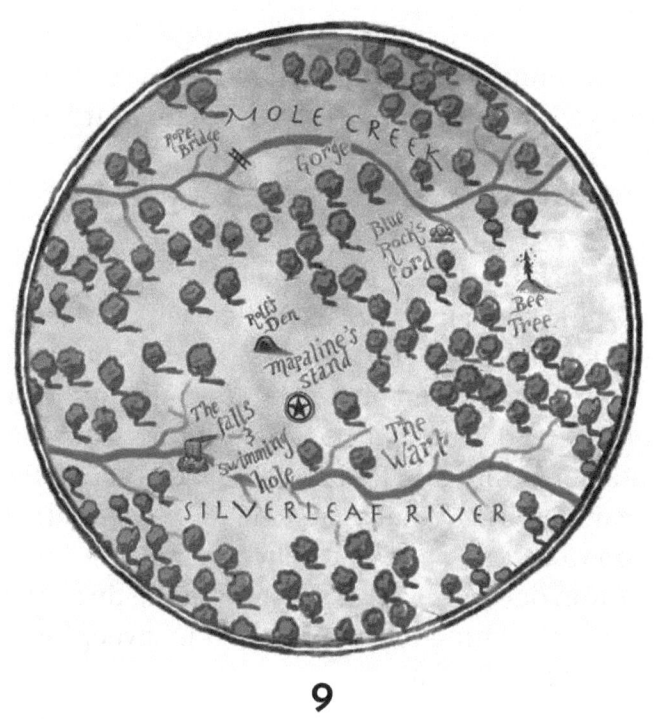

9

The Signal

AUTUMN IN THE Great Wilderness is just as splendid as it is in our world, maybe more so, and is full to the brim with all sorts of wonderful things: there are bonfires and hunting and the traveling merchants' final visit before winter. There's the crisp, cool air, the leaf smell and wood smoke, the cold nights and the warm blankets. In the autumn the green sea of trees turns to fiery red and yellow and orange, like a sunset that lasts all day long.

It was one of Mapaline's favorite times of the year.

But as she climbed over Saela and out of bed this morning, Mapaline felt... well, she felt... blah. Aker had left the day before for an extended hunt—the first he'd ever taken alone—and would not be back for several days. Saela had some chores to attend to with her family, and Red was sick with a cold. All this meant, probably, that Mama Maple would find some extra work for Mapaline to help with and that the crisp, autumn day would pass, not in romping through the woods or fishing in the pool, but in sweeping and cleaning and canning.

Besides all this, she woke to find that her beautiful autumn hair—just as bright and colorful as you might imagine it to be—was beginning to brown.

So, you see what I mean. With the day beginning like this, you can hardly blame Mapaline for feeling blah.

But Mapaline was in for a surprise.

"Mapaline," said her father at breakfast, "you and I are going to leave today for an overnight hunt. Just the two of us."

He said it casually, in his own slow, quiet way, as he passed the butter for the morning's honey rolls. "There are stores to set by for the winter, and with Aker off on his own, I thought it would be a good opportunity for us to spend some time together." He paused. "Mapaline? Are you alright?"

Mapaline had stopped mid-chew and was staring at her father wide-eyed and open-mouthed. She had been on many hunting trips, even overnighters, but never with so little notice. And never with just her father. And never had a day that seemed so dull turned suddenly so exciting.

"When do we leave?" she asked.

"As soon as—" But he never got to finish, for Mapaline was already up from the table and running out the door to get her things.

IT DIDN'T TAKE but five minutes for Mapaline to gather her traveling hammock and a blanket and an extra set of clothes and throw them all into her oversized hunting sack. Onto her belt went her new knife, off the wall came her bow, and into a quiver went a dozen arrows. All this flurry of movement surely woke Saela and turned the neat and tidy bedroom into a whirlwind of clothes and trinkets and supplies, but left her more or less prepared for the day ahead. She threw her new cape across her shoulders and charged back out the door, down the tree and into the living room, breathing hard and smiling so widely that it almost made her face hurt.

I'm sure you know what happened next. Roots never move as quickly as sprouts would like, whether human or treeborn, and though Mapaline was ready to go *right now*, this *very instant*, her father was still chewing his breakfast and drinking his tea. He was dressed for the hunt, but it didn't take Mapaline long to realize that his pack was still hanging on its hook, very much *un*packed, and that he would not be ready for some time yet.

"There's no rush, Mapaline," Mama Maple said. "You didn't even finish your breakfast."

And so it was that Mapaline had to force herself to sit back down, to finger her food, and to watch her father slowly finish his breakfast and clear away his dirty dishes. It seemed to take ages for him to gather his things and string his bow. Ages more for Mama Maple to prepare the food they would be bringing, and just when Mapaline thought that they were nearly ready to go, Saela showed up and had to have all the day's events explained to her.

"Have a wonderful time, Mapaline," she said, and it was really impossible not to return Saela's beautiful smile, no matter what hurry Mapaline felt she was in. "I wish I could come. Mother told me last night that I'm to report to her right after breakfast. From the tone of her voice, I think I'll be doing chores all day."

"All day?" Mapaline asked and then, from the corner of her eye, she caught her father listening closely.

"I don't really know," Saela sighed. "But it was clear she had plans for me."

She slumped into her chair, pouting, but it was mostly for show and she wasn't very good at pretending to be sad. It was not an emotion that suited her. Soon she sat up straight again and began to butter her breakfast. "Maybe you'll see Aker while you're out," she said. "I hope he's very careful, out there all alone and—"

Mapaline rolled her eyes and ruffled her friend's

already very ruffled hair. "Aker will be fine and you can stop worrying about him."

If you have never seen it, I can tell you that when a treeborn blushes, especially a Magnolia, the rose color is really quite remarkable.

Saela squeaked, "Well, all I mean is that—"

"I know what you mean," Mapaline said as she smoothed her friend's hair more or less back into place. They exchanged a look and a smile and that was that.

"Are you ready, Mapaline?" her father said.

Was she ready? Of course!

Goodbyes were said and then down the tree they climbed, packs and bows hung from their backs, and soon they were walking down a well-worn trail to the east. For a while they walked in silence. Papa was quiet, even more so than usual, and Mapaline was content to soak up the cool morning air and the smells of autumn in the Wilderness. There are some people who, when you spend time with them, you always feel the need to fill up the quiet with words, and any lull in the conversation feels awkward and uncomfortable. You don't really know what they are thinking or if they are enjoying themselves or if they feel awkward too, and so you keep talking and talking until you go your separate ways. This is how it often feels with strangers and acquaintances and even casual friends. But then there are others—far fewer, I'm afraid—with whom silence is not uncomfortable at all and you can pass an hour or two with barely a word between you.

This is how it was for Mapaline and her father. Saela,

too, had become such a friend, and Rolf, who sometimes seemed to say more without words than many people do with all their jabberings strung together. Papa and Rolf were very alike in that regard, and maybe that helps explain why Mapaline had loved Rolf so easily.

After a while, though, when their hill was behind them and the sun was fully up and warming the day, she began to feel the need for conversation.

"So, Papa, where are we going?"

"I thought we'd go up to the Wart," he said slowly. "I always like sleeping in that tall oak—the one you children sometimes start Arrows from."

"Me too! Do you think it will be a clear night? It can feel so close to the stars up there."

"I think so," he said, and then they walked on a while longer in silence. By lunch they had reached the Wart and taken up positions in some of the maple trees lower down the western side of the hill. Papa Maple always felt most concealed from game in a maple, and the two settled in close to the trunks where they could see out into the branches while blending in.

If you have ever been hunting, you will forgive me for skipping over this part of the story. Hunting is not terribly exciting to read about. It involves lots of sitting and waiting and thinking and waiting and napping and waiting some more. I will move ahead, I think, to dusk, and by this time they had downed a sparrow each, cleaned them, and washed all the bloody mess from their hands and clothes. You would think that after having done so little they would not be very tired, but the opposite was in fact the case. They were soon high up in the oak at the crest of the hill, hammocks strung and lying back to wait for the stars. The sky was very clear, and the light lingered a while until, almost suddenly, it was dark.

After talking about constellations and seasons and how the moons each found their own course through the night sky, they grew quiet and let the crickets take over.

Then, after some time: "Mapaline, are you asleep?"

"Not yet," she said and yawned.

"Mapaline, I . . . wanted to talk to you about a few things. Will you climb up to the top with me?"

OH DEAR.

Parents have a certain tone, don't they, when they have something serious to talk about. Or something sad or frightening. Papa Maple was using that tone now, and Mapaline remembered the sideways glance at breakfast and that he had seemed more distracted than usual on their hike and wondered if she had been taken out today to be told some particularly dreadful news.

Up they went, to the very tip-top of the tree, and then for a few moments they were quiet again.

"Look," Papa said finally. She could just see his long, twiggy finger held out in the dark and follow it to the valley far below. There was a flicker of light there, dancing at the stream's bank. "That will be Aker, I'll bet," he said.

"Is that why you chose this spot?" Mapaline said. "You're spying on Aker, aren't you?"

"No, I just . . . well, *spying* isn't exactly the right word. I just wanted to . . . um . . ."

Mapaline giggled. "It's all right, Papa. It makes me feel better to see his fire as well." In the dark she could not see her father's face clearly, but she could tell that Papa Maple was smiling. Then, nervously, she said, "What did you want to talk to me about?"

"Yes," he said. "There were two things, really."

Mapaline waited in the quiet as he decided which to broach first. Finally, he said, "I just wanted to tell you how thankful I am for Rolf."

"Rolf?"

"Yes. I was . . . um . . . uncomfortable with him at first. It's not every day you meet a talking animal, and rarer still that he will take a great interest in one of your children. I was protective and perhaps not overly friendly."

"Rolf understands," said Mapaline. She reached out and held her papa's hand.

"I know he does. But I just wanted you to know that I'm very thankful for him. He's a good . . . bear. A good friend. I'm glad to have him around."

Mapaline didn't know quite what to say. She loved Rolf dearly, and in a very different, yet very similar way, she loved Papa Maple. It made her feel warm inside to know that her father approved of her friend and welcomed him.

"Thanks, Papa."

"The second thing, I'm afraid, is some bad news," he said. "I know—"

The Signal

He stopped. Mapaline was still holding his hand and felt his fingers stiffen and tense. Then Papa was standing and climbing up even higher, all the way up to the last branch that was strong enough to hold him. She followed close behind.

"Look," he said. He was whispering, and it made Mapaline nervous.

"What is it, Papa?"

"Look there, up on the horizon."

Mapaline looked to the east and found the place where the bright field of stars disappeared into the dark hills. In the distance—the *far* distance—was a single, yellow point of light standing against the landscape. It was larger than any of the stars and flickered while they remained steady and still.

"What is it?" Mapaline asked.

"I think it's the Tower," he said, and then paused. "I've never seen it lit before. Strange." There was a moment of silence and then, "Weren't you just asking about the Tower? Not too long ago?"

"Yes," Mapaline said. "Rolf said something about it. That he's been there before."

"Hmmm . . . I've never even *heard* of its being lit. Even my grandfather never mentioned such a thing. What else did Rolf say?"

But before she could tell him, their attention was directed toward something more immediately concerning. Down in the valley, far away but still clear in the cool night air, they heard a shout. Then another. And then Aker's little campfire went out in a wink.

Mapaline

IF YOU ARE reading this, I think it's very possible that you have something in common at this point with Mapaline or her father. It seems very likely that you either have children of your own, as Papa Maple did, or a brother or sister, as Mapaline had. In either case, I hope you will immediately understand what happened next. There is something inside us, something deep and strong, that binds us very fiercely to our families, and when a child or sister or brother is in trouble—*real* trouble—this something can come out in a very powerful way. We don't have to think about it. We don't have to consider or plan. It just *comes* and we run as fast as we can to the rescue.

So when Mapaline and her father heard those shouts, and you can bet that they recognized Aker's voice even from so far away, they did not pause to plan what they should do. They did not consider if it was too late in the night to go traipsing through the woods or too dangerous to cross the stream in the dark. They did not wonder, even for a moment, whether or not all this could wait until morning.

They ran to the rescue.

Down the tree, grabbing their bows and arrows on the way. Down the far side of the Wart, staying close, watching out for one another in the dark as they leapt over fallen trees and boulders. Up to the edge of the stream, which was running less deep now than it had been in the early summer, and then quickly across, wading to their armpits in the cold, rushing water. Papa led the way up the bank and straight as he could to the spot where they had seen the campfire. Soon they smelled the smoke and saw the embers still glowing in a little clearing beneath three maple trees.

Beside the remnants of the fire was a dead rat.

"Stay here and be ready," Papa Maple said, and so Mapaline stood on the edge of the clearing and nocked an arrow.

Her father approached the animal very slowly, and though his attention was focused there, he was always looking up and about too, listening for any movement in the surrounding woods. It was a large rat, and its long tail was thick like a snake.

Papa Maple poked it with the end of his bow, and then harder, to be sure that it was really dead.

It was.

"Aker!" he called out, softly at first and then louder, "Aker!" It did not come naturally for the treeborn to shout at night, especially not when they were on the ground where a passing predator might take an interest in them. But the impulse to remain quiet was overcome by their desire to find Aker, and so Mapaline called out as well.

"Aker!"

He was in the maple tree, almost directly above them, and soon dropped to the ground next to the cooling fire.

"What are you two doing here?" he asked, but his voice did not sound as Mapaline expected it to. With the shout and the sudden disappearance of the fire and now the dead river rat sprawled on the ground, she had expected Aker's voice to be shaking, for his fingers to be trembling and for him to be so happy to see them come rushing out of the woods to save him.

But he was none of these things. In fact, Aker actually sounded somewhat irritated to find them here, and Mapaline noticed that he was standing taller and straighter than usual.

"Were you spying on me?" he asked.

"No!" both Papa and Mapaline said at once. Then, "We were out for a hunt, up on the Wart," Mapaline explained. "We saw your fire down here . . . a long ways off . . . and then . . ."

"We weren't spying," Papa said. "Just . . . well . . ." He coughed. "It looks like you had some trouble with a rat."

Aker scowled. "No trouble at all. He surprised me, I guess, the way he approached the fire and came right at me. I've never seen a rat do that before. But I was ready and had my bow nearby. No real danger. I retrieved my arrow and left him for someone's dinner. If you'd waited another five minutes I'd have been asleep up in my hammock."

It was quiet then, but not the same sort of quiet that had passed between Mapaline and her father on the long, pleasant walk this morning. This was rather different.

Papa Maple coughed again and scrunched up his face into a grimace. Then he said, "Mapaline and I will be sleeping up—*way* up—on the Wart tonight. Tomorrow morning I think we'll get an early start for home. The weather looks promising . . . You should stay out a few days longer than you planned, Aker. I mean, if you want to. Come on, Mapaline. It's time for bed."

The Signal

Mapaline started to follow and then Aker stopped them. "Mapaline, if you see Rolf, will you tell him I'm alright? I don't need any babysitters, furry or otherwise."

Mapaline nodded and knew somehow that Rolf would never think of such a thing. Rolf would understand.

"Aker," Papa said. "I'm sorry. Good night."

By the time they got back to their hammocks, Mapaline and her father were very tired.

But neither had any trouble waking up early to head for home.

It was a longer, more tiring hike back to the stand. I'm afraid that both Mapaline and her father were still feeling very bad about the night before. This by itself lent a dreary, gray feeling to the morning despite the blue sky and warm sun. Besides this, their bags were now heavy with little leaf-wrapped packets of meat from the sparrows they'd killed, and the long slopes they had walked *down* to get from their stand to the Wart were now long slopes *up*, which made their legs burn and their feet hurt.

After a while, though, Mapaline's thoughts turned to the Tower and she began to daydream about who might have lit it and what it all might mean. She began to imagine all the creatures who might have once lived there—giants and dwarves and humans—and what they might have looked like and dressed like and done.

But just as her spirits were beginning to brighten, she remembered something else that brought back the gloom. You're expecting it, I imagine.

Her father's bad news.

"Papa," she said. Papa Maple was walking a few paces ahead of her and he stopped to let her catch up. "Papa, there was something else you wanted to tell me last night. You said you had some bad news."

"Oh. Yes." It was obvious that he was not looking forward to sharing it, just as she was not looking forward to hearing it. But some things must be done.

"Mapaline, it's about the Magnolias. I know you've grown very fond of them, especially Saela. We all have. But . . . well, they've decided to leave before winter. The last merchant caravan is due soon, and the Magnolias are going to leave with them and travel south to one of the larger stands for the cold months. There are many magnolia trees in that part of the Wilderness, and they hope to join a stand in the spring."

This was bad news of the worst kind, and I'm afraid, with all that had happened, Mapaline immediately began to cry.

"Why do they have to go? Can't they join our stand? We could help them build. Or . . . Saela could keep sharing my room. I don't mind."

"I know, Mapaline. I wish they could, but Saela's father and the other roots . . . It's hard to understand when you're so young, but the older you get, the more you need to be connected to a tree of your own. Of your own *kind*. I can't imagine not having a maple tree to live in. For your mother and me, no other tree would be the same. We would feel disconnected, like fallen branches. It's a wonder that the Magnolias have stayed as long as they have, but I've seen the longing growing in their roots. They need to move on. To graft in somewhere else."

"But couldn't they just . . . can't they just . . . get *used* to other trees?"

Papa Maple shook his head and pulled Mapaline into a hug. "It doesn't work that way, Mape. It just doesn't. And there are no magnolia trees near here; you know that. So they have to leave. The roots *want* to leave; to find a new home."

"I don't understand," Mapaline said between tears.

"I know. Someday you will."

When something terrible has happened and we don't understand why, this is usually not the answer we want to be given. I'm afraid, however, that it is often the right answer, whether we like it or not.

Mapaline didn't say much for the rest of the morning. When they finally arrived back at the stand, Saela rushed down to greet her and immediately began to cry as well. It seems that her parents had shared the same news with her the day before. So for a while they cried together and then wandered down to Rolf's den, where they cried some more with him. Even Rolf shed a tear or two, not because the news surprised him or because he thought it was a terrible decision, but because sometimes even good and right things can bring sadness.

My goodness. I'm afraid that this story has not ended altogether so nicely as the others. I hope you'll forgive me. You will find that the stories of *this* life do not always end happily, even when they do end rightly. It is a fact. Sometimes, though, the sadness brings a good cry and the good cry lets it all out and then, somehow or other, we begin to feel better. It was, I'm happy to say, the same with Mapaline and Saela. By evening they were laughing again and enjoying each other's company and telling stories at the dinner table. By dusk they were feeling much better and went looking for Rolf again to see if he would take an evening walk with them. Rolf, however, declined.

He, too, had seen the Tower's light and was off to investigate.

Dear Journal,

Rolf is gone and i don't like it one bit. i've grown so used to having him around. Worst of all, i could tell that he was nervous when he left. Well, not nervous. Rolf doesn't get nervous. But anxious all the same. He said that his friend would only signal him if it was very important. And then, after all our goodbyes, do you know what he said? He told me to make sure my boots were well oiled for winter.

Oil my boots for winter? What a strange thing to think of before leaving. it's not very sentimental. But i guess he did get me the boots and all the rest so . . . oil them i will. But really . . . winter's still many weeks away.

                              Mapaline

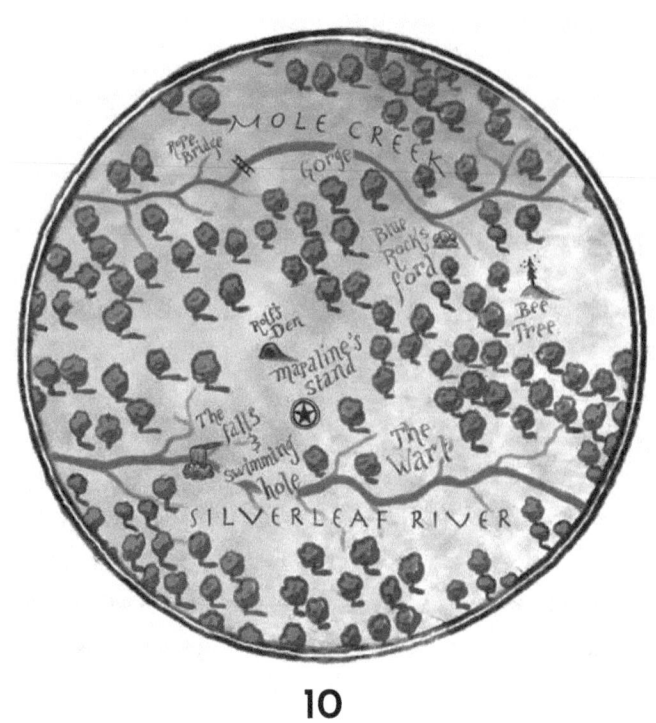

10

Mapaline's Stand

SEVERAL DAYS LATER the weather turned decidedly toward winter. The first frost came early and sent the treeborn of Mapaline's stand scrambling to finish all their preparations for the cold months ahead. All the wood they would need was not yet gathered and the autumn nuts and berries not yet stored safely away. Early cold meant that supplies

Mapaline's Stand

would have to be put aside quicker and last longer, and this led to no little anxiety and stress.

Just a week after her hunting trip, Mapaline was beginning to feel the strain on her whole stand. She'd barely seen Aker since he had returned, and all her friends were so busy that there was no time for playing of any sort. Mama Maple was sharp with Mapaline over silly things and Papa overly distracted. Rolf had yet to return, which was concerning even though she knew that Rolf could certainly take care of himself.

And over all this hung the fact that the merchants would be arriving soon.

The merchants. The singing and dancing and adventurous merchants whose visits Mapaline had always enjoyed would not be so welcome this year, for when they left, Saela would be going with them.

So when Red burst into the high-hung living room of their hometree late one evening to announce that the caravan was approaching, Mapaline sighed and did not rush to greet them as she usually did. Instead, she and Saela exchanged a glance and held hands and slowly went down together.

Mapaline's mood, however, was not the only thing that was different this time around. As the merchants made their way up the north face of the hill, they were moving slowly. Their heads were down. They were not singing. There were three carriages now instead of four, and these looked, like the merchants themselves, much worn and disheveled.

Mapaline found Coco at once, and though they smiled and hugged and greeted one another warmly, there was no denying that the springtime light in the sprout's face had been dimmed in the months she was away.

"What's wrong, Coco?" Mapaline asked. Briar and Nettle arrived and stood near them while the roots from the stand began to help the merchants lift their wagons into the trees. The sky was cloudy and darkening quickly; the wind was cold, and the gloom from the caravan seemed to spread across the hill like a fog. Hardly anyone spoke at all.

"We've had a terrible summer," Coco said. Her voice was tired. "Just terrible."

"What's happened?" Nettle asked.

"We've had . . ." Coco stopped and shrugged her shoulders and shook her head, and now Mapaline saw that her friend was about to cry. So they hugged her, all three of them, and told her not to worry and that everything was going to be all right. Briar ran to fetch some hot tea and was soon back to join the others around a little fire on the green. Aker came up then and Red and several of the other children from the caravan, and over all of them seemed to grow the most terrible melancholy.

Finally, when the visitors had been given tea and the fire was built up to throw more heat against the cold night, Coco tried again.

"We've had terrible storms. Just like the one in the spring when we were here, only some of these were even worse. And bandits. Other *treeborn*, if you can believe it, stalked our caravan for a whole week and then raided us, setting fire to one of our wagons and stealing some of our goods. It was awful. My father said that in all his years of traveling, he's never seen thieves as organized and determined. Then, just last week, a wolverine attacked the camp. It wasn't even the first we encountered this year, but this one broke right into the wagon where Tumble and her family were sleeping. Right in. It just smashed down the door and then . . ."

She stopped.

"Where *is* Tumble?" Mapaline asked, for by now they had realized her conspicuous absence.

Coco just shook her head and all at once Mapaline's heart sank and her breath was stolen away. For a long time, no one spoke.

"And Ceylon too?" Nettle asked. "Was Ceylon . . . hurt . . . too?"

"No." Coco sniffled and blew her nose on a handkerchief that Mapaline handed her. "No, but about a week ago he left us. No one really knows why. One morning we woke to a note that thanked us for all we'd done but said there was somewhere else he needed to be. And he was gone. And now we're not even sure we can make it back home for the winter. So many of our supplies were stolen and the wagons are in such bad shape. My parents are very worried."

Silence settled on them again and then Coco took another sip of tea and one of the honey rolls offered her and wiped her eyes. "I miss . . . I miss Tumble terribly."

Mapaline wanted to do something, to *say* something that would make her friend feel better, but all she and the others could manage was to share her tears. It is like that sometimes, and more often than not, shared hugs and tears are far better than anything else. After Coco's stories it simply wouldn't have been right or even considerate to tell her "It will all be okay" or "Everything will turn out for the best" or "It's not so bad." Sometimes it *is* so bad. Sometimes everything is simply *not* okay and it does no good to pretend otherwise.

One of their friends was dead.

Their other friends, those among the merchants, were in desperate trouble.

And so nothing much more was said that night until the tea was all drunk and the tears all shed and they all whispered "good night" and headed for their beds.

But Mapaline could not sleep, and neither could Saela. They lay there upon Mapaline's little bed, pushed over as near as they dared to her little hearth, staring up at the wooden ceiling of her little room. And they *felt* little and tossed about as the wind moved the tree back and forth.

"Mapaline," Saela said. "I'm scared."

There were easily a dozen things to be scared of tonight, and so Mapaline asked, "What of?"

"It seems like . . ." Saela paused and then propped herself up on an elbow. The glow of the fire shone upon her bare head and lent shadows across her smooth face.

"It seems to me that something is not quite right. Not quite right with . . . well, with everything."

"What do you mean?"

"I never told you this before. I told Rolf, I think, but that's different... It was other *treeborn* who attacked our stand."

"Really? I had assumed it was wolves or something."

"No, it was other treeborn, like us. And now treeborn attacked the merchants as well. Have you ever heard of such a thing?"

Mapaline thought for a moment. All the stories she'd heard around the campfire, of battles and armies and thieves and dangerous journeys, always seemed to set the treeborn against some other enemy. There was the occasional treeborn villain, but usually they acted with an evil troupe of dwarves or ogres. As far as she knew, there were no stories of treeborn attacking or raiding each other in force.

"I don't think I have, now that you mention it," she said.

"And another thing," Saela continued. "Animals have been acting strangely all summer long, haven't they? Who ever heard of a snake stealing necklaces and teacups? A raccoon, maybe, but not a snake. And didn't you say that a rat attacked Aker on his hunting trip? That he came right up to Aker's fire?"

"Yes. And we saw wolverine tracks near the stand last winter, which is unusual enough, but there were two sets right together."

Now Mapaline propped herself up as well. "And speaking of the winter, even old Caddo said he couldn't remember one as cold as last year. And this winter is starting out earlier and colder still."

"And the storms."

"Yes, they *have* been bad."

Both girls were quiet for a moment, thinking and rearranging these ideas around in their heads like parts of a puzzle that they might not have all the pieces for.

Then Mapaline said, "There's the Tower too. That's very unusual."

Another pause and then, both of them together whispered, "Rolf."

"You don't think . . . ," said Saela, and her eyes were wide and truly frightened now.

"If you mean do I think that Rolf is somehow to blame for such terrible things, or even part of them, then of course not," Mapaline said. "But if you mean that all this . . . this strangeness is somehow related, well, Rolf may be the strangest thing of all."

Saela blinked in the firelight and then lay back down, and so did Mapaline. But they were still very much awake, and in time, Saela spoke again. "If Rolf is strange, then I want to be around *his* kind of strangeness all the time. All the time until he seems normal and the rest of the world becomes odd."

"Me too," Mapaline whispered. "Me too."

THE NEXT DAY, as everyone from the stand and the caravan woke and breakfasted together and began the busyness of the day, the mood on the hilltop was dramatically improved. Nothing had changed, mind you. It was still very cold—the ground had frosted again—and there were still more chores to do than might probably get done and the merchants were still battered and grieving. But the sun was now rising instead of setting and somehow this has an effect on people that goes beyond circumstances.

"Good morning, Coco." Mapaline smiled and hugged her friend. She and Saela and Red had brought their breakfast down to share with some of the merchants, and they all sat at tables that had been assembled in front of the three hanging wagons.

"Good morning," said Coco. Then she went over to a nearby campfire and returned with a steaming kettle.

"Tea?" Mapaline asked. "We brought some too."

"Not tea," Coco said as she filled a row of wooden cups. She had the hint of a smile on her face, like she had a secret she was just about to share. This made the other sprouts very curious, and they were soon peering eagerly into cups of dark, black liquid.

"Wait!" said Coco, and into each cup went a splash of cream and a drop of honey. "*Now* try it."

They did.

I'm afraid that Red was not very good at politely hiding his opinions, but Coco laughed at his scrunched-up face and didn't seem offended.

"Well, what do you think?" Coco asked.

"Well," said Saela.

"Hmm," said Mapaline. "It's very . . . strong. And sweet. I think . . . I think I'm not sure. What is it?"

"It's called 'coffee.' Father purchased some from another trader, and all the roots are hooked. I'm with you, though. Sometimes I think I like it and other times I go straight back to tea."

"What's all this?"

The little breakfast party turned to find Aker emerging from the woods to join them. Mapaline thought suddenly that the weather and the animals weren't the only things that had changed over the past year. Aker had too. He was standing taller and walking faster and had an air of confidence about him that had not been there even two or three months ago.

Saela handed him her cup, which he studied and then smelled and then sipped.

"Oh!" he said and then sipped again. "What is it?"

"Coffee," Saela said and refused to take her cup back. "You're welcome to mine. I don't think I like it."

"Thanks!" He took another healthy swallow. "Guess what Thatch and I found down by the stream? Some big tracks. Really big, and neither of us have ever seen them before. Papa and Green are down there with some of the merchants now. Coco, your father thinks they're from a mountain lion."

"We're a long way from the mountains," Coco said, and Mapaline and Saela gave each other a look.

"I'll say," Aker said. He took another gulp of coffee. "My father said to tell you all to carry your bows with you today. And to stay close to the stand as much as possible. Thanks for the coffee."

He handed his cup back to Saela and was off, leaving the rest of them to talk about his news. This didn't amount to a great deal since Coco was the only one who knew anything about mountain lions, and even she didn't know that much. Besides, there was lots to do and breakfast was soon over.

Mapaline's Stand

MAPALINE WAS ASSIGNED to wood-collecting duty for the day. This was not her favorite chore, but Nettle and Saela and Red were given the task along with her and this made the hard work less tedious. All morning long they scoured the wooded parts of their hill, gathering twigs and small sticks into bundles and dragging larger branches to the green where others from the stand would chop them up later.

Then after lunch they went out again to gather more wood.

You can imagine that by dinnertime they were pretty well exhausted. Clouds had moved in during the day and the sky was threatening a cold rain, and since pretty much everyone in the stand had worked just as hard as they had, fireside conversation was cut short and many headed to bed early.

This time Mapaline and Saela had no trouble falling asleep.

Have you ever startled awake in the middle of the night and thought that you heard a bump or clatter from another part of your house? It seems to have woken you, but at the same time it seems as if it might have been part of a dream and so you lie there, listening and trying to sort out what your sleepy mind remembers of the noise.

It happened just like that for Mapaline, only instead of a bump or a clatter, she thought she'd heard a shout.

Mapaline lay there listening. This meant, unfortunately, that she heard all *sorts* of things, things she wouldn't typically notice at all, but now every rattle of the windowpane or scrape of a branch or creak of the wooden boards beneath her bed seemed doubly loud. She tried very hard to concentrate and to sift through all the racket for the shout she thought she'd heard, but . . . nothing.

If you are like me, when I'm in this situation, what I really want is for the noise to have been my own imagination so I can go back to sleep and not worry about it anymore. This is what Mapaline wanted as well, but I'm afraid she didn't get her wish.

She was just about to give up her listening when the shout came again, from outside, and there was no denying it this time. Saela had heard it too and sat straight up in bed.

"What was that?" she whispered.

"I don't know," Mapaline answered, and then they were both out of bed, feet on the cold floor and searching for boots, arms and shoulders shivering until they found their coats, and then Mapaline remembered what Aker had said and they grabbed their bows and a quiver full of arrows on the way out the door.

They did not go straight down to the ground. That would have been very foolish; if there *was* some sort of danger, there was a good chance that the ground was not the place they wanted to be. Instead, they went down only as far as the flat roof of the living room and then stood still to finish buttoning their coats and pulling hats down over their heads and chilled ears.

To their surprise there was a layer of snow covering the stand—the first snow of the year. But the clouds had moved on and the Water Moon's brightness was reflecting off the ground and the trees, so much so that they could see quite a ways into the night. The

Mapaline's Stand

wagons were swaying gently, and next to Mapaline's own tree was Briar's maple, but there were no lights or signs of movement. Mapaline scanned the outline of the central green next, all the way around, picking out the individual trees that she knew as well as you know your neighbors' houses. The moons were so bright in this false dawn that, even when flurries began to drift down again, she could make out Green Fir's tree farthest across the way from her. It was dark as well.

But moving.

A new sound met her ears then, a thrashing and scraping, and she saw the branches of Green Fir's hometree moving wildly on one side. There was the crack of a branch and then another shout and then ... oh, then came the most terrible sound Mapaline had ever heard. The mountain lion's call was strange and violent, something between a scream and a roar, and the sound ripped through the branches and trees of the whole wood.

Then came an answering call.

"Look!" Saela gasped, and Mapaline looked down beneath the nearest wagon. In the darkness she saw the outline of a great cat stalking through the snow. It was enormous. Much bigger than a fox or a wolverine; bigger even than a wolf.

Lights were going on now in the hometrees around them, and there were more shouts and calls as the rest of the stand woke to the noises. Another crack of wood came from across the way, and this time it didn't sound like a branch at all but like the boards of Green Fir's room.

What, I wonder, would *we* have done? Would we

have been brave enough to stand up straight? To string our bow, with cold and trembling fingers? To reach for an arrow and step nearer the edge of the roof, high up in the tree, to get a better shot at the mountain lion that was now up on its hind legs battering at a merchant's wagon and scraping long claw marks down its side?

I hope so. I truly hope so, though I am sure we would have been very afraid the whole time, just as Mapaline and Saela were afraid as they did all those things.

Mapaline shot first, but in the darkness, she couldn't see exactly where the shaft had gone. The lion felt it, of that she was sure, for it immediately jerked and sprang away in a bound, which caused Saela's own shot to miss its mark. For a moment—just the shortest of moments—it lay there crouched in the snow and then it was off again, but not to run away. Whether it had heard the twang of the bowstrings or seen with its cat's night vision, in a flash it was bounding in *their* direction, toward *their* tree, and before they could fire again, it was beneath them, clawing and scraping up from under the room so that they couldn't possibly hit it with their arrows again.

Any number of things could have happened next. Perhaps Papa Maple would have swung out the door and shown the creature what a grown treeborn with a knife and a hatchet could do. Perhaps Aker, who was awake as well and armed, would have had a better angle on the beast from the doorway of his room and from so close could have placed an arrow through its heart. Or perhaps despite all their bravery and courage, the screaming mountain lion would have found his revenge on the two shivering sprouts upon the roof.

I don't know what *would* have happened.

But I do know what *did*.

For an instant, a patch of woods behind Mapaline's tree grew so pitch-night black that all the moonlight was swallowed up in it. Like a deep hole, a cave opening up in the very air, there was no more snow or light or ground, but only darkness. And then that darkness moved through the trees with the power and ferocity of an avalanche.

It was Rolf, and though his fur was black, there must have been something burning far more brightly in his heart, for the roar that came from his jaws may have shaken the whole wilderness. Before the climbing lion could react, it was thrown from the tree and sent sprawling in the midst of the green. Then there was another unworldly cry as its companion leapt from the fir tree to join it, and the two began stalking round and round the bear that advanced on them.

Mapaline hardly recognized Rolf. He was as he had appeared weeks ago atop the snake that had attacked Aker, only now she didn't see a *passing* fury but a settled one. His fur was standing on end and he looked twice his normal size, teeth bared in what was definitely not a smile. The lions circled, one of them limping but both able to dance away and dart back, looking to pounce if only they could get past the huge sweeping claws that knifed through the air.

By now Mapaline and Saela and undoubtedly a dozen other treeborn had nocked their arrows and taken firing positions atop all their rooms and from windows and doorways all around the stand. But it was too dark and the movements too quick to risk hitting their friend, so instead of helping they could only watch and wait and hope for an opening. They waited and waited, but the opening did not come. The lions moved as though they knew they were being watched, and just as they would step into a clear patch of moonlight, they would dart back quickly toward Rolf's flank, never near enough to be struck but always so close to the bear that none of those in the trees could fire safely.

It seemed like hours passed but, at the same time, in their memories the treeborn would often recall how quickly this all took place. The lions, pacing and circling and testing, seemed to be closing in, and then, in a flash, both lions leapt at once, large and powerful in their own right, screaming all the way.

One landed on Rolf's broad back but the other, the unfortunate other, Rolf caught in midair. With a roar that made their calls sound like a kitten's purr, he slammed the creature to the ground and stomped it once with claw and foot, so deeply into the earth that the impression would last long after the body had been dragged away.

Then Rolf's cry turned to one of pain as the claws upon his back found their way through his thick coat of fur, but Mapaline's arrow flew straight and steady, and though it was a small thing, the painful distraction was enough. Rolf twisted violently, throwing the second lion to the ground with enough force to slide its weakened body across the snow.

Mapaline's Stand

And then, lying in the open, a dozen more arrows finished what Mapaline had begun.

THE NEXT MORNING, after the damage had been assessed and the lions had been dressed and cleaned, there was a meeting. Green Fir was unhurt, though one wall of his room had been smashed in, and several roots had already been hard at work repairing his hometree. All the stand gathered on the central green along with the Magnolias and the merchants and Rolf, who was not hurt too badly and lay in the snow to keep Mapaline and her friends warm.

It was decided that, with the winter setting in so early, the merchants could not continue on toward their homes in the south. So they, and the Magnolias too, would stay until spring.

It was a somber moment. Food would be tight, to say nothing of space, and the roar of the lions still seemed to hang in the air like the threat of more to come, but at the news Saela would be able to stay longer, Mapaline could not help feeling glad. She and Saela were sitting in the crook of Rolf's great arm, and she hugged her friend and Rolf snuffed them both with warm bear breath that nearly blew them over. Then Aker came over and knelt by Saela, and though neither of them said anything, Mapaline saw her friend smiling again, in a different way, and didn't mind at all.

Later that day, things got more or less back to normal. The new normal, anyway. There was now the need for even more winter provisions than usual, but there were also far more hands to help in the work. Rolf stayed close all day and helped as he could. He promised a deer or two when his back was healed, and by evening Green, Moose, and Papa Maple decided that with all the sleep the stand had missed last night, there would be an early end to the chores and extra rest for all.

Which meant that Mapaline could finally spend some time alone with Rolf.

Several fires had been lit around the green and they found a place near one of them to lie down. It was really about the most comfortable thing you can imagine, far more comfortable than my favorite recliner at home or even your cozy bed. Mapaline was near enough to the fire to keep her front half warm, but instead of her back half being chilled, as is always the case when sitting around a fire, she buried it in the thickest, warmest fur blanket that there has ever been. All the warmer, for it was still attached to a very cozy, very comfy bear.

Most everyone else had gone to bed when Mapaline said, "Rolf, I didn't like it when you were gone."

"Neither did I," he said.

"Thank you for saving us."

"Saving you? Hmm . . . yes. Well, thank *you* for saving *me*."

Mapaline laughed at that and snuggled in even deeper. If she was still, very still, she could feel Rolf's great heart beating beneath her.

"You would have been fine, Rolf," she said. "Nothing can hurt you."

There was a grumble and a rumble, a thoughtful mumble, from inside him that vibrated to the tip of her nose.

"Rolf?" she said.

"Yes, Mapaline."

"Please don't ever leave me. I want to be with you always. All right?"

She knew it was a silly thing to ask, a childish thing, and she expected him to say something about her becoming a grown-up someday or that his *heart* would always be with her or something like that.

Instead, she felt his breath on her face and his rough tongue on her cheek and he said, "Yes, Mapaline. Always."

And that was that. He didn't promise and she didn't ask him to because, really, it's only people who break their word who need to make promises. Those who keep their word can be trusted to simply do as they say.

A few moments passed and Mapaline was thinking about this and then Rolf said, "Mapaline?"

"Yes, Rolf."

"Will you walk with me? I'd like to talk a while."

"Of course, Rolf." And they did.

Dear Journal,

i've just gotten back from a very long walk with Rolf. He told me . . . goodness, he told me so much. i could write pages and pages! But i'm far too tired. Honestly, i can barely write straight, so i'll have to add more later. But . . . i have some decisions to make. Some very difficult and confusing and serious decisions. Decisions i can't make until i've slept, so . . . good night.

Epilogue

ROLF AND MAPALINE walked and talked many times over the next week. Rolf told Mapaline all about his trip to the Tower and what he had discovered and much, much more, for the time of secrets had passed.

Then, when all that could be told was told, he took a walk with her papa and mama that ended around a fire back at the stand.

"What do you mean, Rolf?"

Papa Maple's voice was still slow and still soft, but there was something else in it now. A nervous pitch. An anxiousness to match the face that Mama Maple was making.

Rolf was lying on his belly with his arms crossed and his nose toward the flames. The first snow had gone, but the cold remained and the grass was beginning to trade its summer green for the dull brown of the colder months. As if on cue—and perhaps it *was* on cue—Mapaline came up to join them.

"I need Mapaline to come with me," Rolf said. "On a long journey. Something has happened."

Epilogue

"What's happened?"

"The Tower has been lit. It is the signal for us to come. My friend... *friends*, really... are waiting for us."

Papa and Mama looked at Mapaline, who stood near Rolf with her hand on his side and an expression on her face that they had not seen before. A serious expression.

"But," Mama said, "What are you going to do, Rolf?"

"There is an enemy. An enemy of the Wilderness. Of everything. Haven't you noticed? The harshness of the winter? The restlessness of beasts? The violence of your own kind? The enemy has come down from the north, from the lands beyond, and I need Mapaline to come with me to help stop it."

"By yourselves?"

"No." Rolf began to smile and then stopped. He was really getting quite good at catching himself, and it wasn't a moment for smiling anyway. "There are others."

"Will it be dangerous?"

"Yes," said Rolf.

"How long will you be gone?"

"I don't know. A long time, probably."

"But, Rolf," Mama said. "Why do you need *her*? She's just—forgive me, Mapaline—but she's still a sprout. How can she help you?"

"Why have you chosen *her*? Why not find a soldier? A warrior?" Papa asked.

"She was chosen because she is *not* a great warrior, I think," said Rolf. "But it was not I who did the choosing. At least, not really; I have only drawn the thread, not woven it."

"I don't understand, Rolf."

"Do you need to?"

"Of course!" said Papa Maple, and now his words were not so slow and not so soft. There was fear in his eyes, and love, and sometimes those two emotions are very close friends. "Of course we need to understand. We can't just send our only daughter off blindly!"

"Blindly?" asked Rolf. His eyebrows scrunched. "Do you trust me, Papa Maple?"

"Yes, we trust you, Rolf, but—"

"No, Papa Maple," Rolf stopped him and rumbled. "I mean, do you *know* me? Do you really *trust* me?"

Papa looked down at the fire and the silence lasted for longer than was comfortable. Then finally he said, "Yes. We trust you."

"Then it is not blind. Trust me when I say that she is *needed*. That I will be with her. That all the good that she could ever hope to have lies on this path and not up in her safe bed in her safe hometree. Trust me. That is not blindness."

There was a long pause and Mapaline watched as her parents looked at Rolf and then at her and then, holding hands, at each other.

"Mapaline," Papa said finally. "You're not *really* a sprout anymore, are you? Though your mama and I might have trouble seeing it. Do you want to do this?"

Though she had already made up her mind, days ago when she and Rolf first talked about it, Mapaline's head was still swirling. She didn't understand it all either. Not *all* that Rolf had explained to her, not

Epilogue

exactly where they were going, or *exactly* what they would find when they got there. But she knew enough. She knew Rolf. Yes, *she knew Rolf.*

"Yes," she said, and Mama Maple started to cry.

Papa stood up, and for just a moment he glared at Rolf as no one had dared to glare at him before. But then he said, "Very well. Let us help pack your things."

Dear Journal,

Tomorrow Rolf and i leave the stand and head east for the Tower. i've never been so frightened and excited in my life. i've never felt so grown-up and so much like a child. it's very confusing, but . . . i'm ready.

i'm ready for whatever lies ahead, just as long as Rolf is with me.

Mapaline

The End

(for now...)

About the Author

RYAN SOUTHWORTH LIVES in Cincinnati with his wife, Kyna, and their two children. In addition to his writing schedule and parenting, Ryan teaches History, Literature, and Latin through a large homeschool co-op.

Ryan's other work includes *Descending* (Amazon, 2019), a dystopian science-fiction novel perfect for young adults. Reviewers touted this read as "intriguing, thrilling, gripping, unpredictable, and artfully written." In addition, Ryan has had several short stories published online.

Ryan earned two bachelor's degrees from Baptist

Bible College in Scranton, Pennsylvania, in both Bible and secondary education with an emphasis in social studies. Additionally, he earned a master's degree in English with an emphasis in creative writing from Northern Kentucky University, in Highland Heights, Kentucky.

When not teaching, he considers a morning spent at a coffee shop writing to be just about the best way a morning can be spent.

From the author:

"*Mapaline* began as a short story for my daughter when she was very young. She liked bears and I love the woods and so . . . there you go. One story turned into two and three and eventually additional stories began to merge and link together into a loose novel that took place over one year in Mapaline's life.

By the time *Mapaline* was born, my daughter was older, by about eight years, but thankfully she still loves bears . . . and *Mapaline*."

The Enchanting World of the Treeborn Trilogy

EMBARK ON AN extraordinary journey with the Treeborn Trilogy, where a tapestry of adventure, captivating characters, and wondrous new creatures awaits you and your family! A masterful blending of the strange and familiar, this is a story that will spark your imagination and keep you wondering and wanting more!

> Book 1: Mapaline (Arriving Spring 2024)
> Book 2: Ceylon (Unfolding Fall 2024)
> Book 3: The Last Tower (Landing Spring 2025)

Written for readers of all ages, the Treeborn Trilogy combines whimsy and depth in a narrative both delightful and profound. Perfect for a lazy summer day or as a lyrical read-aloud for the whole family, everyone will be left wanting "just one more page!"

If you found joy in the magical realms of Narnia or Middle Earth, or if your kids loved *The Green Ember* or *The Wingfeather Saga*, their next obsession is sure to be *The Treeborn Trilogy*.

Available on Christianbook.com, Amazon, through the publisher, the author, or your favorite local bookstore.

The Treeborn Trilogy Team

THE TREEBORN TRILOGY is the product of a team of dedicated professionals for whom we are extremely grateful and wish to give credit:

Author: Ryan J. Southworth
Illustrator: Adam Watkins
Project management: Molly Turner, Leslie Turner
Copy edit: Julie Breihan
Cover and interior design: Jonathan Lewis
Author photography: Mark Lopez
Publisher: Encourage Publishing

Encourage Publishing has multiple imprints, including *Encourage Books, Encourage Music, Encourage Kids, Wildfly, Turner Creative,* and *Alienta!* Learn more about Encourage Publishing, our titles, and our submission requirements at www.encouragepublishing.com.

BROOK HANDLE RIVER

BULL RIVER

LAKE GREENTIDE

THE GREAT WILDERNESS